KELLY M

THE FEELING GOOD CLUB

SAY
HOW YOU
FEEL,
ARCHIE!

ILLUSTRATED BY
JENNY
LATHAM   LiTTLE TiGER
LONDON

This journal belongs to:

ARCHIE!

Welcome to your journal!

There are spaces all the way through to share the feelings you have experienced each day. You can use this page to create some of your own emojis to add in to your journal! This will help you to see how your feelings change day by day (and moment by moment!). Have fun, and enjoy finding out more about yourself and your feelings!

Happy... Elated... Excited... Unhappy... Frustrated...

Angry... Enthusiastic... Upset... Disappointed... Proud...

All about you!

My name is:
Archie. Well, Archibold actually, which means 'genuine, bold and brave'!

My eyes are:
Sort of browny greeny, like Mum's

My hair is:
Mainly keratin (over 90%!), which is a fibrous, helix-shaped protein. And also red!

Hobbies I love:

I love Science Club and Chess Club, which are both at school, and hanging out with my dad, when we get any time together! And learning about space and dangling my little brothers upside down over the sofa, if that counts!

My favourite food is:
Spaghetti with olive oil and cheese and peas, with tomato ketchup. I don't know if it's actually a thing with a name or if Dad made it up. He calls it Spaghetti à la Archie!

My best friend is:
Well, it's best friends now because there are two of them — Shazmin and me have been besties since Year 3, and now Bella's joined in too! She helps calm us two down, LOL!

My motto for the year is:
Never tie your shoelaces in a revolving door. JOKE! OK, a sensible one is: do your best, be yourself, hide your fruit pastilles from your little bros!

Day of the Week: Tuesday

Feelings I experienced today:

Tuesday, 6.22 p.m., after tea — I've escaped to my room!

Ah, at last! Some peace to do my final prep for the Science Fair tomorrow! I've had no time to myself since I got home from school! First I had to help my brothers draw cartoon dogs, then play Uno with them, and now they're bouncing around on space hoppers downstairs – they've made an assault course around the kitchen!

Mozambique

If Mum were here she'd say *NO WAY* to that, of course, but she's on another research trip – this time to Mozambique for eighteen weeks, which is over four months! She's a marine biologist and it's all about seahorses at the moment – her last trip was to Cambodia!

NO WAY!

Dad *did* say *NO WAY* but then he had to go on a Zoom call with people in America for his new business, so Ed and Amos forgot and started up again. Then *I* said *NO WAY* and I added *OR I'LL PUT YOU TWO HEAD FIRST IN THE WHEELIE BIN AND PUSH IT SO YOU ROLL ALL THE WAY DOWN THE HILL TO THE FISH AND CHIP SHOP!* But they obviously thought I was joking because they just laughed and then Ed bounced Amos off a massive cushion pile (built from all the cushions on the sofas in the sitting room).

I wonder what velocity a wheelie bin could reach if you pushed it really hard? Hmm, I might have to do some experiments on that! So, anyway, I escaped up here – you've got to choose your battles, right? Especially when you're second in command of the regiment, like I am at the moment, until Mum comes home!

I really miss her – she's been away for seven weeks now. At least being so busy at school and looking after the minions (that's what I sometimes call my little bros!) does take my mind off it. They're six, and twins, and super hard work. I just wish Dad had a bit more time to hang out with me – between him being so busy and there being no one else to look after Ed and Amos, it feels like we never get a chance to talk. And when we do, he's always checking his phone and it seems like his mind is somewhere else. *UGH!*

11

So, back to telling you about the Science Fair... Hang on, there's no *YOU* to tell, *LOL!* I'm just writing this in my Feeling Good Club journal, so no one's going to read it, are they? I never imagined writing a journal but I'm really getting into it. Bella got hers first, and she said writing stuff down really helped her understand her feelings when she was going through a hard time with her best friend Rosh moving away. That's when me and Shaz started hanging out with her, and we've been a three ever since. That's also when we created the Feeling Good Club. During Feeling Good Week we did a mindfulness activity session with a lady called Kris, making glitter jars. We enjoyed it so much we decided to start a club to try out the other activities in the handout Kris gave us. We started with baking cookies and mindfully eating them – that one was *YUM!*

So, about this journal ... it does feel a bit funny

writing to myself. Like, *hello, me*! But I like it.
I like the whole thing of having my own private
space to think in and to write whatever I want
to. I'm probably not going to write lots about my
feelings, like Bella does. Instead, I'm going to write
proper reports of the activities we do, and I'm
also going to write about *SPACE!* Learning about
space is my favourite, *favourite* thing of all. Dad's
really into it too, and it's been *OUR* thing ever
since I was about four and he first took me to the
Science Museum. It's something I'm passionate
about, and finding out more about it makes me
feel really good.

I think I love space so much because it makes me feel really, really small and like I'll only be here on Earth for a tiny blink of an eye. That might not sound like a great thought but actually it does really help if I start getting worried or anxious about anything. It makes it not seem to matter so much, in the grand scheme of things. It also feels totally magic that this planet here where we live is actually part of *SPACE!* It's amazing! We are basically living in space, if you think about it. I mean, *WOW!* It's so mind-blowing, how could I *NOT* be totally obsessed with it!

So, of course, for the Science Fair, I'm doing my exhibit about *SPACE!* There are about twenty of us in Science Club and we're putting on this big exhibition in the hall. We were allowed to choose whatever topic we wanted, because Mr Krzysik, our teacher, said that the whole point is to share whatever we're most passionate about, because being passionate about something is what really

14

Earth

Mars

helps get other people interested in it too. The whole school is coming to look at our exhibition a couple of classes at a time, and then the parents are coming before pick-up to see it too. Dad's going to absolutely love it! We haven't been to the Science Museum since Mum's work trips started as there's no one to look after Ed and Amos. Getting babysitters for them is *NOT* easy, *LOL!* And now Dad's running his own business, he often has to catch up with work on the weekends. Between that and Mum being away, things definitely aren't as much fun as they used to be.

Saturn

Anyway, my Science Fair exhibit is about whether there's really life on Europa, which is Jupiter's 'blue' moon. Jupiter has seventy-nine moons – well, that's how many have been found so far! Imagine that! You'd be just standing on Jupiter going, "There's a moon, there's a moon, there's a moon," like, seventy-nine times! I mean, if you *could* stand on it without being instantly

Sun

frozen to death and just crumbling into icy dust immediately. Although, how many you could see before your frozen eyeballs dropped out of your face is another question.

That's the question I asked Shazmin and Bella today when they were helping me finish off my model of Europa at lunchtime.

"Oh, Archie! That's disgusting!" Shazmin cried, very dramatically. Which is not unusual – she wants to be an actor when she's older and she does *everything* very dramatically!

"I reckon you could see twenty-four of the moons before the frozen-eyeball thing," said Bella, with a giggle.

I was really pleased that they wanted to help me today, because I had quite a lot left to do and time was running out. Usually Dad would love getting involved in things like this, but I've ended up doing most of it by myself. I thought he would drop everything to create a moon of Jupiter out of meringue with me because he loves baking, but he's been so stressed out with work that he didn't have time. He just ended up popping into the kitchen to put the two halves in the oven for me – and to comment on the mess I'd made, obviously!

Europa is one of Jupiter's four largest moons, and it's only slightly smaller than our own moon. Awesomely, scientists think there could be an actual *OCEAN* under its thick, icy crust. We're all having our own stand (well, table!) at the exhibition and the centrepiece of mine is the model, and I've got an information display too. Working out how to make the model was tricky, because I wanted to show the icy crust, which is probably a few kilometres thick, but also to show the subsurface ocean that may be beneath it. Like, *WHAT?* How amazing will that be if it turns out to be true? I wonder if we'll ever be able to find out, by getting a space bot to dig down under all that ice!

So, to make my Europa, I experimented with papier mâché round a balloon, but it was taking too long to dry, so I tried Polyfilla, but it cracked. I was getting a bit desperate by then, and I started thinking outside the box, but Dad said *NO WAY* to using toothpaste and trying to harden it with a hairdryer (spoilsport!). Then I had another think, and because I love baking, I tried meringue, which worked!

First, I whipped up a ton of it, following a recipe (I love measuring everything to the exact gram on the electric scales!) and baked it round two metal mixing bowls. Then I stuck the halves

1 Whip up meringue

together to make the icy crust of the moon. I made it so you can take the top half off to see the (possibly actually there) subsurface ocean underneath. My ocean is in a glass mixing bowl half full of water with cling film over the top – handily we had one a little smaller than the metal bowl, so it fitted inside the lower half of my meringue moon perfectly.

2 Bake over mixing bowls

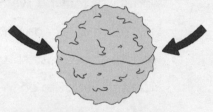

3 Two halves together make icy crust of moon

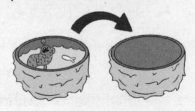

4 Remove section to view ocean

In version one it was a clear balloon with water in but I ended up with a flood all over the table! That's the thing about being a scientist – you have to be prepared to take risks and experiment. I did point that out to Dad when he was trying to

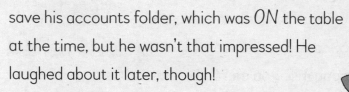

save his accounts folder, which was *ON* the table at the time, but he wasn't that impressed! He laughed about it later, though!

So, anyway, when Bella and Shazmin were helping me at lunchtime today, Shazmin actually – *GASP!* – asked me an interested question about what I was making, which was: "Well, is there or isn't there an ocean under the ice?" She probably wondered because she was expertly turning out little tinfoil fish to go in it.

"No one knows for sure yet," I said, feeling pleased to be asked. "The Galileo mission, which was launched in nineteen eighty-nine, sent back lots of information about Europa and the theory is that there is a subsurface ocean, so it could contain life forms," I explained. "But probably they're more likely to be microbes than actual fish, which is just as exciting to scientists, according to my book by Stephen and Lucy Hawking."

Shazmin wrinkled up her nose. "Microbes don't sound very exciting," she said. "And definitely not as much fun to make." She picked up a jar of eco-glitter. "Although, we could use this for microbes – bling up the ocean a bit!"

"No way!" I cried. "One thing I bet it definitely *isn't* is glittery."

Shazmin did a twirl and struck a dramatic pose. "Everything in life is better with a bit of glitter," she said. "As long as it's the biodegradable kind, of course!"

Bella giggled. "If no one's actually sure what's in the only-probably-existing ocean, then I'm going to make you a massive sea monster." She reached for the green crinkly film in the centre of the table.

I really wanted to go "nooooo!" and make them stick to what is scientifically likely, but I couldn't

resist the thought of people
lifting off the icy layer to
find a really cool scary sea
monster staring at them.
And I *knew* it would be really
cool because Bella is totally amazing
at art. I also knew that when Shazmin gets an
idea about something, it's far better just to let her
get on with it than argue, so she went wild with
the glitter. At least now, when I talk about the
microbes, I'll have something to point at!

While we were working away we got into this
chat about whether or not we'd go into space if
we had the chance.

"I definitely wouldn't," Shazmin said. "There's
no Drama Club in space, for a start, and none of
my mum's paneer dosas and no Netflix."

"And more to the point, no toilets!" added Bella.

"There are toilets, actually," I said. "They cost
twenty-three million dollars and you wee into

a kind of space hoover part that sucks it into a container, and then it gets recycled into drinkable water because that's better than bringing up clean water from Earth."

"Ugh, how is that better?" groaned Bella.

"And what about a number two?" giggled Shazmin. "Surely there's not a vacuum cleaner for that!"

"Well, in that case—" I began, but they didn't want to hear any more, for some strange reason, *LOL!*

I'd love to go into space. Hey, I know, maybe my whole family could go together – by the time I grow up we might be able to stay in a space hotel on the moon, and it would be just like going on holiday, except your ice creams would float about...

Actually, can you even *get* ice cream on the moon? I bet you can... But do freezers work in space? Hmm, I'll have to check on that one.

Oh, hang on, Dad's knocking on my door...

7.44 p.m., still in my room.
So Dad came in to give me my clean laundry and I said, "Do freezers work in space?" because that's what was still on my mind.

Dad smiled. "Great question. There are cryogenic freezers which boost the biological research capacity of space shuttles."

I grinned. "So not for ice cream then, unless you want some sort of alien life form in with your mint choc chip?"

Hi!

Dad laughed, and said, "I love the way your mind works. Never stop being curious, Arch, or wondering about things.

SCIENCE FAIR

It's easy to forget all the wonders of the universe when you get older and there's so much life stuff to do!"

"You're still coming to the Science Fair tomorrow, though, right?" I asked him, feeling suddenly anxious.

"Of course. I wouldn't miss it for the world," he said. "I bet you're the only Science Club member in history who has made a meringue moon of Jupiter with a thick, removable, icy layer and a hidden ocean underneath!"

"I bet I am," I told him. "And it's now also got a scary sea monster and a load of fish and glitter microbes too, thanks to Bella and Shazmin."

Dad laughed again at that. "Well, that's scientifically highly improbable!"

"I know!" I said, with a big, fake sigh.

"It's great you've got such good friends at school, Arch," Dad said then, sitting down on the edge of the moon. (No, he didn't somehow rocket into the sky at that moment! I've got a really cool moon and stars duvet cover.) "When I was your age I didn't really have that – I spent a lot of time on my own," he added.

"Is that why you created a clone of yourself to hang out with?" I joked. Me and Dad are so alike – everyone says so – and I look like a mini version of him. Sometimes I even mess around, calling him a time-travelling older version of me! "And, yes, I'm glad I've got Bel and Shaz too," I said then. "It was already great having Shazmin as a best friend, but now Bella's joined in, it's

brilliant – she kind of calms things down between us. And I can't wait for our next Feeling Good Club meeting on Thursday." Just thinking about it gave me a rush of excitement.

"Oh yes, you're making a start on the

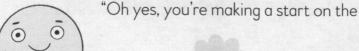

clubhouse, right?" Dad asked.

"Yeah, Bella's dad's going to help us repair the old summerhouse at the bottom of their garden," I said. "It's the perfect base for our club."

Then I got a sudden great idea – a way for me and Dad to spend more time together. As I said, we haven't been able to hang out much lately. "Hey, why don't you come and help out too?" I suggested. "You've already booked Ed and Amos into after- school club, so you could come straight over to Bella's. It'll be really fun and I'm sure Bella's dad would love an extra pair of hands."

Dad frowned and my stomach dropped. "I'd love to, Arch," he said. "But I booked the extra childcare so I could catch up on all the orders that came in this week. I really, really have to get them processed. I'm sorry. Another time, yeah?"

"Sure," I said, giving him a smile and trying to hide my disappointment. I know it's not Dad's fault, and I'm really pleased his business is going

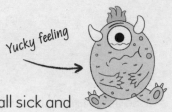

Yucky feeling

well, but my stomach felt all sick and churny at the thought that he couldn't find the time for me. I felt like a balloon with all the air let out of it suddenly, but I didn't want to bring us both down, so I quickly changed the subject. "Did you know that Europa's crust has distinctive markings in the form of dark stripes," I said, "which may be ridges formed by eruptions of warm ice at an earlier stage in its life." I'd learned that off by heart from my book, for my little talk that goes with my exhibit.

Luckily Dad didn't seem to notice that my mood had dropped. "I can't wait to hear the whole thing at the Science Fair tomorrow," he said. He smiled and ruffled my hair.

I was about to ask if I could practise my talk with him, but just then two things happened at once – one, Ed and Amos started having a

28

massive row right outside my room and two, Dad's phone started ringing in his office downstairs. He leaped up and made for the door. "I have to grab that," he said. "Could you—"

"Yeah, I'll deal with these two," I told him. Then loudly, I added, "I reckon, for every second this fight continues, that's a day without TV or the PS4..."

"I reckon so," said Dad, giving me a grateful smile. Then he bounded down the stairs, leaving me to referee.

Ed hung off my hand and swung about, whining. "Archie, don't say that about the TV because it's not my fault. *He* started it."

Amos grabbed my other hand and started swinging too, while sneakily trying to kick Ed. "That's not true – *he* started it," he wailed. "He always starts it."

"Hey! Stop kicking me!" cried Ed then, and tried to kick him back.

I sighed. As usual, they seemed to have forgotten what the argument was about and instead were focused on who started it!

"Right, no more arguing and no more kicking," I said sternly. "You know, I wish I had super-strength so I could lift you both up with one hand and throw you out of the window. Just – boom – straight out. That would serve the pair of you right!" Obviously, I was joking, *LOL!*

"You wouldn't!" cried Ed, giggling.

"We'd tell Mum and you'd get no TV for a million years," added Amos.

"Hmm, you might be right. I suppose I'll just have to tickle you then!" I cried.

I threw them on the bed and leaped on them. At least tickle fights take their minds off arguing with each other, and they are kind of fun for me too!

Dad was ages on the phone, so I got the minions changed and made sure they did their teeth and read them a story. Then, before they went to bed, we all spoke to Mum on Zoom. Ed showed her the dinosaurs he made out of Lego, and she wished me loads of luck for the Science Fair tomorrow. Dad's promised to take tons of pictures of my stand, so she can see how amazing it looks.

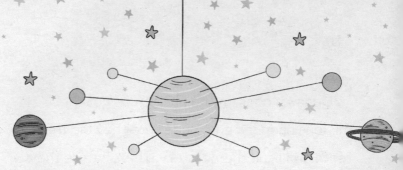

After we all said goodbye, Dad put the minions to bed and I came back up here and I've been writing this and chilling out under my light-up solar system.

I've been waiting for Dad to come and say goodnight, but I can hear he's in another Zoom meeting he had to do for work. It's gone on way longer than he said it would! Oh well, I'll have to just tuck myself in and say goodnight to myself, I suppose. Goodnight, me! I hope I can sleep when I'm so excited about the Science Fair tomorrow!

Day of the Week: Wednesday

Feelings I experienced today:

Wednesday after school, 3.51 p.m. — back in my room with the door SHUT!!

Well, I don't feel like writing anything in this stupid Feeling Good Club journal now because I'm feeling *REALLY BAD!* I still get a sick feeling in my stomach when I think of the Science Fair. I don't want to write about what happened. *UGH!* But I can't think about anything else either! Maybe it will help if I get my feelings down on paper, like Bella does. I can't keep feeling as *AWFUL* as I do now so I'm going to give it a try.

OK, well, before it all went horrible, it was brilliant, so I guess I'll write about that first. For the first two hours each year group got thirty minutes to come round our stalls and I got to do my talk over and over and everyone thought it was so cool and tons of people asked if they could eat the meringue. I said *NO!*, of course.

It was brilliant watching each little group that gathered round my stand pull off the ice layer and find the ocean underneath – they all loved Bella's sea monster!

She and Shazmin hung around with me for a bit when it was our year's turn to go round the whole fair, and that was really fun. Shazmin never listens to anything I say, usually, but she said she was really impressed with how lively and interesting I made my talk on Europa.

But then the YUCK happened. It was an hour before home time and the bit where the parents were invited in. Loads of grown-ups filed in right away, but Dad wasn't there. I thought he'd just be parking the car but it got later and later and ... ugh, I don't even want to write this, but after twenty minutes there was still *NO DAD!*

I had to keep smiling and doing my talk but I kept glancing at the clock on the wall of the hall and watching the door expecting him to appear. I was thinking *there's only twenty minutes left*, then *ten*, then *five*. At that point I started worrying that something bad had happened to him. Mr Krzysik even came over to see if everything was OK – he must have noticed me looking at the clock a lot. I had to tell him that Dad hadn't turned up, but I acted all

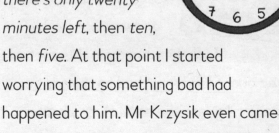

cheerful and said that he was probably just stuck in traffic.

Then it was time to pack away, and there was still no Dad... My legs felt a bit shaky then and to be honest I actually wanted to cry, but I didn't want everyone to see how upset I was. I did ask Shazmin's mum Keerti to take some pictures of me with my stand (she helps out in the library listening to reading on a Wednesday afternoon). So that was something anyway, but I don't look very happy in the photos!

She asked about Dad and I had to tell her he hadn't come yet. I guess she or Mr Krzysik must have gone and said something to Mrs Crossfield, the school secretary, because a few minutes later she came and told me she'd given Dad a ring,

and he was sorry, he'd completely *FORGOTTEN* about the fair and was on his way right now!

She gave me a really kind look and said, "Don't worry, Archie, this happens to at least one person at every single school event!"

It was so nice of her that I felt even more like crying, especially when she added, "You can leave your stand up until your dad gets here and show him then if you want."

I didn't, though – I didn't want to be the odd one out and have everyone asking me why I'd left it up, so I packed it away while everyone else was doing theirs.

All the Science Club members went home with their parents and carers straight after the fair, but I had to go back to class. As I sat down next to Bella, she whispered, "Are you OK, Archie?"

"We just saw my mum in the corridor, and she told us what happened," added Shazmin, leaning over our table.

"I'm fine," I managed to mutter.

"Course you're not," Bella whispered, squeezing my arm. "I'm really sorry. You must be so disappointed. But, you know, sometimes these things just happen. Your dad couldn't help forgetting, and it doesn't mean he wasn't really keen to see your exhibit."

"I know," I said. But inside I couldn't help feeling really cross and upset with Dad. My stomach was churning and I felt really sick again, but I also wanted to shout and stomp about, and maybe just burst out crying. How could he have forgotten? He knew how important it was to me. At home time I went out to the playground with my class as normal. Usually we tell Mr Lacey we can see our parents and then go over to them, but before I could get away, Dad came rushing over.

"Oh, Archie, I'm so sorry I missed the fair!" he cried, in front of almost my entire class.

"It doesn't matter," I mumbled, trying to drag him away. "Let's just go home."

"But we can go and see it now," he said, looking really upset. "Mrs Crossfield told me you'd leave it up."

I pulled him across the playground, and Ed and Amos came sprinting over from their teacher to join us. I felt like I might actually be sick, or shout, or cry, and I just wanted to get home and get in bed and curl up under the covers and stay there forever. I didn't do any of those things, of course. Instead I forced myself to say, "I packed it all away. I didn't want to be there by myself."

Dad looked even more upset then. "Archie, I'm

so, so sorry—" he began, but I just dropped his hand and walked ahead of him. I didn't want to talk about it any more.

On the way to the car my bros were trying to throw each other's school bags in the road and I made a big thing of telling them off and then wrestling them into the back seat to keep myself busy. Then when we were driving home, I just looked out of the window so that Dad wouldn't notice me nearly crying. He was really upset too and he kept saying how sorry he was and, as I didn't want him to feel bad, I kept saying it was OK.

But really it wasn't OK. I was desperate to get up here to

my room and be on my own. Writing it all down has actually helped a bit, but I still feel totally *BLEUGH!* How could Dad forget, however busy he is? I still don't get it.

Oh no, I'm being called for tea. I have to go downstairs, even though I still feel really upset and not like eating at all. I hope Dad doesn't bring it up again as I definitely do not want to talk about it any more! And – *UGH!* – I've just remembered – Mum's going to Zoom with me specially to hear all about how it went and then I'm going to have to tell her what happened…

Still Wednesday, after tea. I do feel a bit better now…

Dad had made my favourite dinner – spaghetti with olive oil and cheese and peas – and written "sorry" splodgily in tomato ketchup across the bottom of the plate.

That made me smile a bit and I did actually end up eating most of it. Once we'd all sat down he helped my brothers cut theirs up so we didn't have to watch them slurping it into their mouths!

He said sorry a lot more and I said, "That's OK," a lot, even though it sort of was and it sort of wasn't. When he was washing up and I was drying up after dinner, we got chatting and I did tell him all about the exhibition and about how much everyone had loved my model.

"I'm so, so sorry I missed it, Arch," he said again, for about the thousandth time.

"It's really OK," I said then, and it was almost true.

"Will you do your talk for me now?" he asked, once everything was put away. "I could make us hot chocolate..."

So he did, and I went through the whole talk again, just for Dad. Well, half of it, anyway. Ed came in with a carpet burn he'd done sliding down the stairs and then Amos got upset about there being no biscuits left in the tin and then Dad's phone rang and he had to get it, because it was work. But the half we did was good. Shazmin's mum had sent Dad the pictures she'd taken and so we looked at those too, and at my model. Then we

sent the pictures on to Mum and I got my own Zoom with just her, so no Lego dinosaurs poking me in the head! I had to do the whole talk again for her too, and this time Dad fended off the minions and so I got through all of it!

I really do feel better about the Science Fair now. I know Dad wouldn't miss something like that on purpose, of course I do.

Day of the Week: *Thursday*

Feelings I experienced today:

Thursday, 8.02 a.m., before school.

I woke up this morning feeling much better about the Science Fair thing, and also excited about going to Bella's house later – well, her garden!

It will be brilliant fun to get started on turning her old summerhouse into our Feeling Good Club clubhouse. I've packed some old clothes to take with me because I reckon we'll be getting mucky! There's loads of cleaning and clearing out to do before we can start putting in the furniture or anything like that.

I've made a list of everything that needs to be done, which is:

- Clear out the inside
- Paint the outside
- Take up the rotten floorboards inside and on the porch bit and replace them
- Beg and borrow furniture to fill it with
- Run an outdoor extension cable to it so we can have electricity for my star projector on the ceiling

So not too much to do then, *LOL!* Just basically everything! At school the other day we also made a wish list of furniture and things we want to go inside, and we're all going to have a look at home to see what we can scrounge. Our list said, if I can remember it all:

- Sofa
- Big cushions for the floor
- Rug
- Chest of drawers or SAFE for our secret club

stuff (like one of us is going to just have a spare safe lying around the house, LOL, but you never know!)

- Star ceiling projector (I'm bringing that!)
- Mini fridge and SodaStream (yes, I know it's unlikely but you've got to dream big...)

Our vision →

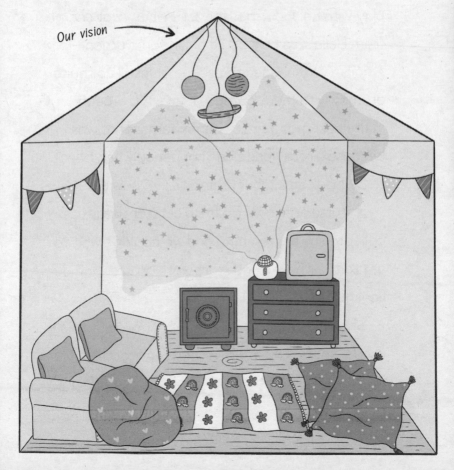

Thursday, 7.16 p.m., getting some peace and quiet at the bottom of our garden — FINALLY!

I really wanted to write in here sooner, but I had to play with Ed and Amos for ages when I got back from Bella's, so Dad could finish some urgent emails. I've managed to escape at last! I got quite grumpy with them because I have *NOT* been in the best mood since I came home. That was because a really bad thing happened when I went to Bella's today ... but I think it's OK now.

It started off fine. Bella's big sister Jess collected us from school and we couldn't wait to get to their house and start work on creating our Feeling Good Club clubhouse.

Shazmin's mum had dropped off a load of half-used paint tins from when they redecorated, so we had loads of colours to choose from. We got

changed into our old clothes, and Bella brought
out some cookies she'd made – *that* wasn't the
bad thing that happened, obviously – so OK, it
wasn't *ALL* bad!

Shazmin was really impatient to get started,
so Bella and I ate cookies as we watched her
painting patches of the different colours on the

outside of the
summerhouse,
which is made
out of wooden
planks. I can't
remember
them all but
I know there
was egg-yolk
yellow and
sky blue and
deep purple

and a vivid pink. At first we were just going to look

at them and then choose a colour, but actually it looked amazing with the planks all multicoloured so we've decided to do stripes using them all! It's also a great idea because it will use up all the old paint – so cheaper *AND* better for the planet!

We did have to stop Shazmin from just painting the whole thing right then, though, outside and inside, because it wasn't exactly ready!

"Erm, Shaz," I said as she started opening yet another paint tin. "I know you're keen on the arty bit, but we have to clear the place out first, then do the repairs..." The summerhouse was falling down in one corner, where ivy had got in and pushed the wooden panels apart.

"And we have to clean it really well," Bella added. "Erm, I think you just painted over a spider..."

"What? Where? Where is it?!" Shazmin cried. "Oh! Is it on me?!" She dropped the paint pot and leaped around, brushing her arms down and shaking her legs about.

"Oh my goodness!" Bella gasped.
"I was only joking!"

Shazmin calmed down after
a moment and breathed a deep
sigh of relief.

I couldn't help grinning. "So you didn't know
about Shaz's fear of creepy crawlies?" I said.

Bella grimaced. "Obviously not. Sorry!"

Shazmin smiled a wobbly smile. "It's all right.
I do wish I could get over it, though. It's a bit
embarrassing sometimes – I can't even bear
absolutely tiny little things!"

At that moment, Bella's dad Steve strolled
down the garden with his toolbox. He'd left work
early to come and help us.

"Hey, guys!" he said cheerily. "How's it going?
I'm so happy you want to transform this place
into something useful. It would be a shame for it
just to fall down!"

We all said hi and Bella gave him a big hug and offered him a cookie.

"Wow, Bella, yum!" he cried, taking a big bite. "These are amazing!"

"Thanks," she said. "I experimented with changing the raisins to chocolate chips and adding orange essence."

"Well, I'm always happy to try out your inventions!" he replied. "Delicious! So, there are several rotting boards that need to be replaced in the floor," he said, helping himself to a second cookie. "Who fancies giving me a hand?"

"If it involves having a go with the crowbar I'm in!" I said, feeling really excited. "And maybe I can do the screw gun when the new boards are down?"

Steve laughed. "Maybe. If you're careful." He turned to Bella

and Shazmin. "Any other takers?"

"I'd like a go," said Bella, but Shazmin just wanted to get on with cleaning the outside walls so she could get the colourful stripes painted as quickly as possible.

"OK," said Steve. "We'll give you a shout when we're ready, Bella."

So Bella got on with clearing out the old junk from inside, and Shazmin went indoors to get some soapy water and cloths. Steve and I went to his car and carried in the new floorboards he'd bought. They were really heavy and we had to transport them one at a time.

As we went back and forth to the car, I told him all about wormholes and time travel, which he sort of already knew about from a podcast he likes.

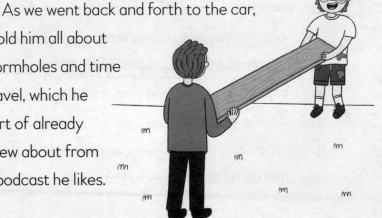

He really listened and asked me loads of great questions, and I found out that I know even more about it all than I thought I did. By the time we'd finished, Bella had emptied everything out, apart from the heavy things that needed two people to lift them. I volunteered to do this with Steve so we could carry on our great chat, and Bella went to help Shazmin with cleaning the spidery bits off the walls and the flies off the windowsills. Apparently they freak Shazmin out as much as spiders, even when they're dead! In fact, *especially* when they're dead!

Imagine! Zombie flies!

Everything was great at that point – me and Steve were like a real DIY team! Once we'd lifted out the heavy stuff we started work on the floorboards and ... well ... I don't honestly know what happened, but something strange just came over me. Bella and Shazmin were listening to our space chat, and making jokey comments about how they didn't understand what we were talking about, and I started to feel really angry and upset for no reason. It felt like I had a rumbling volcano inside me about to erupt and I was trying to hold it down.

I tried to ignore it and be my usual self, but when Bella asked Steve if it was her turn for a go with the screw gun, this torrent of fury just came out of me – from nowhere! "No, *I'm* doing it!" I snapped. "Steve said *I* could." Ugh, I feel really embarrassed writing this now! It really surprised me and I've never done something like that in front of any of my friends before. Well, probably when I was really little, of course, but nothing that I remember.

"There are plenty of boards, you can all have a go," said Steve, jumping in to diffuse the situation.

NO, I'M DOING IT!

Then he had to go to the shed to have a look for some more screws, so it was just us three. I got on with pulling up the last board, wrenching at it with the crowbar with all my might. When it came loose, I looked up and found Bella staring at me.

"What's the matter?" she asked.

I shrugged and said, "Nothing," but I sounded really grumpy and it was obvious she was pretty upset by my outburst.

"She was only asking to have a *turn* with the screw gun, Arch," said Shazmin. "She wasn't taking the job away from you."

I felt really, *REALLY* embarrassed then, and put on the spot, and I found myself snapping, "It's nothing to do with you, Shaz. Why do you always have to stick your nose in?"

"Wow! Moody much?!" huffed Shazmin. Well, *that* just made the volcano inside me boil over completely.

"*She* can do stuff with her dad whenever she

wants!" I shouted, pointing at Bella. "I'm only here for a few hours. Why can't I do the planks with Steve on my own and have a proper chat with him without you two listening in and making fun of me?!"

And before I knew it, I dropped the crowbar and stormed off! Yes, me! Like I said, I honestly don't think I've ever done anything like that before! I mean, Shazmin's stormed off on me at least twenty times in the last couple of years, but it's just not an Archie sort of thing to do. I was absolutely furious, though – I was shaking all over and breathing really hard, a bit like a raging bull!

Shazmin called after me but I kept going, heading for the wooded bit at the back of the garden. Then I flung myself into the hammock with my face turned towards the trees. I was hoping they'd just leave me alone, but they didn't, of course. Instead, they followed me, so I curled up into a ball.

"Have we done something to upset you?" asked Bella. I didn't turn round to look at her but she sounded really hurt. I curled up even tighter.

"Why is spending time with *Bella's dad* so important to you?" asked Shazmin.

That's when I finally understood what I was upset about. I turned round to look at them. "It's not," I said, blinking back tears. "I want to spend more time with *my* dad." I shook my head – I was starting to feel really silly then. "I'm sorry," I mumbled.

"It's OK, Archie," said Bella, giving me a quick smile. "But you have to tell us what's going on. We're a club, and we're your friends. You should be able to share anything with us."

"Anything!" cried Shazmin dramatically. "Your deepest fears and biggest worries and your most furious … furiousnesses!"

I shrugged. "Maybe. But unlike you two, I find it hard to talk about my feelings." I swung my legs over the side of the hammock and tipped myself out. "So, anyway, we should be getting on with…"

They both just looked at me, and I knew they weren't going to let me get away with *that*. I groaned and fell back into the hammock. "Fine, I'll try to share how I feel," I mumbled.

And I guess secretly I really wanted to, even though I also wanted to run away to Siberia and live with a pack of huskies so I didn't have to deal with complicated human stuff. But I couldn't go round bottling things up and then exploding on my friends in a mean way, so if that meant sharing, then, *UGH*, I had to give it a go.

So then Bella and Shazmin got in the hammock too, and we all swung it back and forth a bit and I somehow found the words to tell them how I've been feeling lately, with Mum away for months at a time, and Dad always working or having to look after my little brothers. And how me and Dad never get to do anything just the two of us any more. And how even when we do get time to chat in the kitchen or something, my brothers always come and mess it up somehow. Either that or Dad's phone goes, or he's doing emails and messages at the same time as we're talking. And about how things being like this with Dad makes me miss Mum even more...

"You know your dad would love to spend more time with you, Arch, don't you?" said Bella, when I'd told them everything. "It's not that he doesn't want to. He just can't at the moment."

I made a kind of *gurnururgh* noise like you sometimes hear from the rings of Saturn (yes, they actually make amazing sounds!).

"How about telling him how you feel?" Bella suggested.

Well, even thinking about that made me want to be sick! "No," I said firmly. "I don't really talk like that to my dad, you know, about feelings and stuff."

But Bella clearly wasn't going to give up on the talking idea. "Well, how about talking to your mum about it?" she said then.

I grimaced. "I don't want to worry her while she's away."

"I'm sure she wouldn't mind," said Bella. "She'd want to know if there was something the matter,

and maybe she can help."

"Yeah, and maybe she'd talk to your dad for you," Shazmin suggested.

"Hmm, maybe," I said, but I wasn't so sure. "The thing is, it's not really *private*, even when it's just me and her – my brothers are always running in and out and wanting to show her things."

"Oh, I've got another idea!" cried Shazmin suddenly. "If you can't find time together in the house with your dad, maybe get *out* of the house together." She said it as if it were really simple. For a moment we all just stared at each another – maybe it was!

"But out of the house where?" I wondered.

We were all quiet, thinking, and then, "Aha!" cried Bella. "I've got it! How about going wild camping together? Jess does that with her dad all the time and they love it. They get to spend proper time together, just the two of them, away from screens and stuff."

I wasn't sure at first, because I'm not the most outdoorsy person. But then Shazmin said, "Yeah! Imagine, the two of you having fun putting up the tent together, and cooking beans or whatever, then sitting round a campfire, then getting all cosy in your sleeping bags and sticking your heads out of the tent flap to look at the stars..."

As soon as she mentioned stars I was in! But then I remembered Ed and Amos and all the enthusiasm drained back out of me. "We can't," I said, with a sigh. "My brothers would have to come and then it'll just be chaos and I still won't get to spend proper time with Dad."

But my friends weren't giving up that easily. "What about your uncle James?" asked Shazmin. "He's back from New York for a while, isn't he? Couldn't he look after the minions? He was brilliant with them when he took us all to the cinema that time – he even got them to quieten down when they started acting out the movie in the aisle!"

"Maybe," I said. "I could ask him." I started feeling a bit more like the idea could work, but then an image flashed up in my mind really clearly – of Dad saying no because he quite often catches up with work on the weekends. I told the girls about this, but it didn't seem to put them off.

"You could keep the trip a secret and make it a surprise for your dad," said Bella.

"Yeah, then he won't have time to find any reasons not to go!" added Shazmin.

"Mmm, do you think that would work?" I wondered.

"Totally," said Shazmin.

"Definitely," said Bella.

"OK, well, I'll ask Uncle James and see what he says," I said then. I was definitely feeling a bit more cheerful.

"Great!" said Shazmin. "I declare this an official Feeling Good Club plan! The Surprise Camping Trip."

"OK ... it's a plan!" I said with a big grin on my face. "And I'm sorry again for getting so angry with you guys before."

At that, they both threw themselves on me and gave me a huge hug, and the hammock nearly tipped us all off. "That's OK," said Bella,

NO worries, mate!

and Shazmin said, "No worries, mate," in an Australian accent because she likes to practise different ones.

"We can start work on the plan right now!" Bella said. "Let's go in and get a drink, and Jess can fill you in on everything you need to know to create an amazing wild camping trip. Then we'll have to get back to work! That clubhouse is not going to fix *itself* up!"

And so that was exactly what we did. The bad thing kind of turned into a good thing in the end and I felt so, so, sooooooo much better after talking through my feelings with my friends. I hadn't realized how bottling it all up was affecting me. I feel lighter and more full of fun now – back to the usual Archie! And I love having a secret Feeling Good Club plan to put into action!

So, back to the clubhouse – we worked really,

really hard on it and did loads! We got most of the painting done once we'd wiped down the walls – with us three plus Jess and Steve helping, it was really quick! We had to leave the top bits because we didn't have a stepladder, so Steve is going to see if he can borrow one to finish it off. The paint has to dry properly before any furniture can go in. Bella and Shazmin have managed to get some things for inside, which they're bringing on Saturday. No mini fridge or SodaStream yet, though, *LOL!* But even empty, you can already imagine how great it's going to look when it's finished!

Oh, gotta go – it's time for us all to talk to Mum.

Later, after tea — which I helped cook, by the way. Well, microwave! Star son award for me!

I've talked to Uncle James! I called him
on Whatsapp while Dad was in his office
working. The Surprise Camping Trip is
OOOOOOOOONNNNN!!!!! It's going to happen
next weekend. Woo hoo! And guess what – even
more good news – me, Shazmin and Bella are
going to do a practice camp out in Bella's garden
this weekend, on Saturday night, so that I can
learn all the wild camping skills I'll need from Jess.
Awesome! My friends are being so brilliant! I told
Dad we were having a sleepover in the clubhouse.
We'll be right beside it in a tent, though, so I don't
feel like it's telling a lie.

    We're planning to have a Feeling Good Club
meeting when we get to Bella's – the first one
in our new clubhouse! It's my turn to choose the
activity from the handout Kris gave us. I've gone
for Listening in Nature.

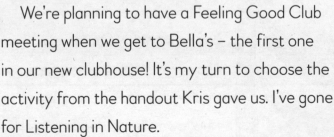

    Bella's not keen on sleeping outside because
she's scared of spooky noises so I'm super

grateful she's willing to do it for me. She's so kind helping me prepare for the trip with Dad. I really want to help her out too, so I've got a great plan to cure her of her fear.

And, guess what? I've got an even *greater* plan to help Shazmin get over her terror of creepy crawlies! So the wild camping practice will be really good for them, as well as awesome for me! It will be brilliant if I can light a fire, and cook on it, and put up a tent, and forage for wild food, and it's all stuff me and Dad can do together! Or

maybe we'll ditch the tent and go *completely* wild, sleeping in hammocks or a yurt made of branches... Oh, I know... I saw something awesome on a TV show once. This guy hollowed out a dead camel he found while travelling across a desert and slept in that...

OK, maybe not! I doubt the girls would be up for it, or Dad, even if I did somehow manage to find a dead camel... which is unlikely seeing as camels aren't native to this country, *LOL!* I am so into the Surprise Camping Trip now! Bring it OOOOOOOONNNNN!

Friday, after tea, in my room.

I'm so excited about our practice camp out tomorrow that I've got everything ready already, *LOL!* My rucksack is packed and I've got my sleeping bag out. When Bella told her dad about the Surprise Camping Trip, he offered to take us tracking in the woods tomorrow – how cool is that? So we'll be looking for animal prints and learning how to recognize which is which. It'll be a great thing to show Dad when we're on our trip – another fun thing we can do together, as well as putting up the tent and making a fire and toasting marshmallows and stargazing and—

Oh, gotta go! I promised to do my brothers' story time tonight and they're calling for me!

Feelings I experienced today:

Saturday night, I don't know the time exactly — we're having our practice camp out!

I'm all cosy by our campfire in Bella's garden, writing this, and the girls are watching a movie on Shazmin's iPad in our tent – they couldn't do without tech for one night! Jess will be back soon – she's gone to sort out the ingredients for our firepit calzones. (OK, so maybe we're not exactly surviving on our own in the wilderness ... ha ha!)

Tonight has been absolutely brilliant so far! Me and Shazmin got here at exactly five o'clock because we were so super keen to get on with the camp out. We put our stuff in the clubhouse right away. It's looking really cool now – the different-coloured stripes still need finishing off at the top, but as most of the painting's done and all dry, Steve said we could get the furniture in. We've got a rug and a huge beanbag-sofa thing from Bella's loft, and a load of sequinned cushions which Shazmin brought over. Bella's mum has even put some pots of purple and blue flowers on the porch so it looks really cheerful. We went inside and after we'd all chatted for a bit, I took charge (well, someone had to, *LOL!*).

"OK, I call this meeting of the Feeling Good Club, with added awesome practice camp out, to order," I said. We put on our club badges that Shazmin had made us, and then I turned to Bella. "Password?"

She stared at me blankly and then giggled. "Uh, I have no idea, Arch," she said. "Wasn't it something to do with a rhinoceros?"

"I'm pretty sure it was about bees," said Shazmin. *RANDOMLY.*

What?! It was literally nothing whatsoever to do with bees!

"Can't you just tell us, Arch, and then we can say it?" asked Bella.

I folded my arms. "What's the point of having a secret club password if I just tell it to you?" I replied.

Shazmin raised an eyebrow. "What's the point of having one when we all know each other and there are only three of us and we can all see we're all already here?"

Bella rummaged in her bag and pulled out her Feeling Good Club journal.

"We have a secret club password because we have a secret club," I said. I mean, obvious, right?

"Sneezing Monkey," said Bella triumphantly. "I wrote it in my journal."

"Argh!" I yelled, leaping to my feet and jumping up and down. "What is the point of having a secret password if you're going to write it somewhere obvious?!" I did some more jumps and arghs to make them both laugh, although I didn't mind really, to be honest. I just love that we have our club, and that I've got such great friends. I still think about what Dad said – that he found it hard to make friends at school. I feel so lucky to have Shaz and Bella, even if they are super argh-making sometimes!

"Sneezing Monkey," yelled Shazmin at about a million decibels, loud enough for the whole

ACHOOOO!

neighbourhood to hear.

I did some more arghs and jumps, and yelled, "What's the point of having a secret password if—"

"If people loudly shout that it's a *secret password*," finished Bella.

I couldn't help laughing at that. "Oh yeah, fair enough," I said, doing a zipping-my-lips sign. "OK, so for our activity today, I have chosen—"

"Please don't tell me it's something to do with science," groaned Shazmin. "I bet it is. Not Schrödinger's Cat again. A cat can't be alive and dead at the same time, not even an imaginary one. That's impossible, end of. You know, Arch, sometimes scientists can really overcomplicate things."

Oh my goodness, sometimes I'm actually speechless with Shazmin! I should take her to a top physics conference – she'd have all

77

the best scientists in the world in tears of despair!
"No, actually it's Listening in Nature," I said, pulling
Kris's handout out of my bag.

"Oh, fine, that's easy, just *listening*. I can
definitely do that," said Shazmin breezily.

"Really?" I asked. "Because, you know, to *listen*
you have to stop talking first."

"Ha ha!" said Shazmin, and playfully stuck her
tongue out at me.

Bella was looking it up in her own handout. "Oh,
and then we can create poems about what we
hear," she said. "Amazing. I'm going to write mine
straight into my journal and decorate it."

"I'm writing mine on a piece of paper and
handing it in for the Home Achievements board,"
I said. "I want perfect grades in my school report
and English isn't my best subject, so this will help
achieve that."

I thought the girls would be super impressed,
but they were *NOT, LOL!*

"Arch, I don't think the point of the Feeling Good Club is to *achieve* stuff," said Bella.

"It's to help us understand our feelings and know how to help ourselves feel better," said Shazmin.

"Especially if we're frightened or worried," said Bella. "For example, I wonder if there's anything in here to help me with my fear about camping out tonight!"

She started leafing through the handout, and Shazmin went to look over her shoulder. "Or about how to get over a fear of creepy crawlies," she added. "They're bound to come scuttling into the tent later on..." She turned pale just thinking about it.

"It's my turn to pick the activity and we're doing Listening in Nature," I said firmly. "The idea is that being outside in nature, and tuning into the present moment, helps you feel grounded and calm. So that should help you handle any spooky noises, Bella. It also gets you deeply connected with the natural world around you, which I bet includes being at peace with creepy crawlies, Shaz. And anyway, because I'm such a great friend, I have already come up with fantastic ways to help you both with your fears, which I shall reveal later on." I glanced at my bag, tucked away in a shady corner of the clubhouse – I had everything I needed to help with Shazmin's fear in there already.

"OK, OK," said Bella, putting down the handout. "You're in charge, Arch. What do we do?"

So then I looked at the instructions. "'Find a comfortable place to sit out in nature and take twenty minutes to simply be still and listen,'" I read out loud. "'Let the sounds wash over you as you breathe slowly in and out of your belly. When you've tuned in to the sound in general, you can start to listen to the different noises, one by one. You might hear birds chirping to one another, wind blowing through rustling leaves, running water or a motorbike revving its engine. Quietly begin to write down the sounds you hear in your journal.'"

Taking our journals with us, we all picked a different place in the garden to go and sit. Of course, it wasn't exactly like being right out in the wilderness, but there were plenty of sounds, which I hadn't even noticed before I started properly listening.

I heard Shazmin giggle a few times from under her tree, but then she settled down. I honestly can't explain how amazing it was, just actually *listening*. I closed my eyes for a while to help me get settled and breathed down into my belly like the instructions said. Then I started listening. Like, really listening. It's funny, because I think I listen all the time when I'm outside, but it's completely different when you just do that and nothing else. It's like floating in a swirl of sounds, and feeling like part of everything.

Hee hee heeeee!

81

The grass was rustling, and the leaves were
making this kind of swishy whooshy noise in
the tree above me. Quite a few different birds
were singing, and when I opened my eyes I saw a
squirrel. I tried to focus on listening for any noises
it made rather than just looking at it.

Someone started up a lawnmower a few
gardens away, and there was an aeroplane
somewhere, faintly roaring, and a woodpecker. I
heard some different bird calls and I recognized
the coal tit's song. We have them in our garden

and every year they nest under our eaves. I'm planning to find out what the other bird calls were too – I bet there's an app or something for that. After a bit, I picked up my journal and started writing, without hardly even thinking about it. Wow, if only English could always be that easy!

We all gathered back in the clubhouse and I could immediately sense how much calmer we were. "You know, it's strange, but I already feel less anxious about sleeping outside, even though I wasn't thinking about that," said Bella. "Just because I've spent some time properly breathing and listening to what's going on around me, instead of turning my 'what ifs' over and over in my mind."

"I do feel more grounded," said Shazmin. "As in, less all over the place and not as up in my head as I usually am! Plus I wrote something literally amazing. I am *literally amazed.*"

We took it in turns to read our poems and all of them were really good. Bella's was quite long, more like a story, and we got really caught up in it, until...

"Hello!" cried Steve, bursting into the clubhouse. We all jumped in surprise ... and did a double take!

"Dad!" gasped Bella. "What's with the leaves?"

"And the make-up?" asked Shazmin.

Steve was wearing a kind of crown of branches, and tons of green face paint. "It's camouflage," he said. "I'm going to take you into the woods, to show you how to track animals, remember?"

Bella grimaced. "Yes, but I didn't think you meant disguising yourself as a tree," she said, clearly very embarrassed.

"I look like a survival expert," said Steve. "Don't I, Archie?"

"Yep," I said.

"Archie, don't encourage him!" Bella groaned, and put her head in her hands.

Luckily for Bella, her mum Kate appeared in the doorway. She took one look at Steve and said, "You can't go like that. If you leap out on anyone walking their dog in the woods you'll give them a heart attack!"

Steve sighed. "This is what we'd do if we were surviving in the wild, and you'd be very grateful when I caught us something to eat!"

"I'm sure I would, love, but still!" said Kate.

Steve shook his leafy head and tutted, then strode off back to the house.

Bella mouthed "thank you" to her mum and

Kate gave us a wink and breezed out after him.

Ten minutes later Steve was back but without the camo, and we set off for the woods. It was brilliant. We found loads of dog tracks, of course, but we were pretty sure some of them were a fox, actually, because, as Steve explained, they were smaller and more elongated. Even without the camo he turned out to be a brilliant guide, and we also found badger tracks and something that definitely could have been a rat's prints.

"A rat? Where?!" Shazmin shrieked, when we spotted those! So she's not too keen on rodents either, *LOL!*

Bella sketched them all in her journal and Shazmin took photos with her camera. I made a list of everything Steve said we might see (we didn't have any luck with the deer prints, even though we know there are deer around here). I also marked each sighting on a simple map that I drew. It was really good fun, and so was driving

86

there and back with the music on full blast. (It was especially funny when Steve started doing wild, pretend headbanging and Bella had to tell him to concentrate on the road!) I know Bella finds her dad embarrassing sometimes, but he was brilliant fun, and he said how great we were to hang out with too! I didn't feel jealous of Bella any more, though – I can't wait to have loads of fun with my own dad when we go wild camping!

As soon as we got back to Bella's, it was time to set up camp. We did loads and it all went brilliantly. I'm even more excited now! My hand is totally aching from writing all this but I'm just going to quickly write what we did in a list:

1. We put up our tent. Jess was going to help us with this, but she'd gone shopping, so I read the instructions and did it all by myself. I wanted to be sure I knew what to do on the wild camp out with Dad, so we could do it together without him having to teach me (and maybe he doesn't even know *how* to put up a tent!). Meanwhile, Bella and her mum made the dough for our firepit calzones, which is like pizza but folded in half with the fillings in the middle, so it's easier to cook over an open fire. Shazmin was "busy" creating a dance routine on the clubhouse porch (no, I have literally NO IDEA what that had to do with our camping practice, but never mind, she said it was urgent!).

2. We put out our bedrolls (mine was borrowed from Jess) and sleeping bags in the tent and got it all ready — and of course Shazmin insisted on going in the middle. Bella put fairy lights

everywhere and Shazmin emptied a whole load of sequinned cushions out of her bag, like the floor cushions she's donated, but smaller, and she's planning to take these ones home again! (I'd been wondering why she had so much stuff!) They were not very sleeping-in-a-hollowed-out-camel, but I didn't complain.

3. Fire lighting — Jess was back from the shops, so she came out and helped us make a fire. She showed us how to lay the wood and kindling in the firepit so it burned well. She talked to us about how to safely make a fire on the ground if you don't have a firepit. That was helpful for the wild camping trip, but it had to stay in theory only because Bella's mum said absolutely no way to digging up half her lawn so we could practise that safely, LOL! I did draw a diagram in my Feeling Good Club journal, though, to help me remember.

I was the one who got to light the fire and it was so brilliant to see the flames take hold and the logs all go up in a bright blaze. I really loved it – it was one of my favourite parts of the whole thing.

In a minute, we're going to make and cook the firepit calzones with help from Jess. That is the last thing on my wild camping preparation list. Like, *actually* on my list. I wrote one out and I've been ticking the things off it. After that, everything will be done and I'll be on my way to wild camping success so that me and Dad have the most amazing trip. OK, gotta go – yummy firepit calzones and wild camping victory time!

Still Saturday night.
WHAT A DISASTER! The camping trip is RUINED and I may as well NOT BOTHER

and Dad's going to think I'm **COMPLETELY HOPELESS**, because if it all goes like tonight he's going to be **COLD** and **HUNGRY** or even possibly **ON FIRE** and **HUNGRY**. ARGH!!!

Still Saturday night, back in the tent with Shazmin and Bella.

OK, my friends have calmed me down a bit (actually, a *LOT*!) and now they're watching a film on the iPad together. I did a *tiny bit* storm off after all the disasters happened ... and that's when I wrote that shouty bit before this part. Hmm, that's two storming offs now! I feel so upset and not like my usual self at all at the moment. I know I sometimes feel stressed out when things don't go as I planned, but this was more like angry-upset again. But I guess anyone would feel angry-upset if:

1. Their firepit calzone fell IN the fire and got cremated.

Whoa!

2. When they were trying to get it out, by spearing it on a stick, they got burned by an ember and ended up pitching the on-fire calzone straight into their friend's mum's flower bed and setting fire to her bark chipping and destroying a lavender plant.

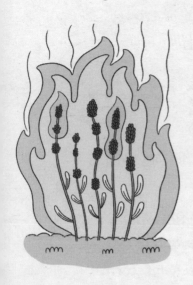

3. After feeling totally awful and embarrassed and wanting to crawl away into their tent, they *did* crawl away into their tent, only for the tent to fall down on their head because they had not read the last page of the instructions, about pegging it down.

PEGS

Heeelp!

4. Then they got stuck in the collapsed tent and had a sort of panic about it and ended up rolling around on the ground drowning in sequinned cushions, yelling and needing to be rescued.

When Bella got me out of the tent, Shazmin saw the state of me and giggled. I know she wasn't being horrible or anything (well, I know that *now*!) but at the time it just made me feel as awful as I could possibly feel.

"Stop laughing at me!" I shouted. "As if you could do any better!"

"Oh, Arch, sorry!" she said, looking a bit shocked.

"Are you OK?" Bella asked me.

"Everything's ruined," I grumbled, feeling the angry-upset volcano erupting inside me like last time. "I can't get anything right. The wild camping

93

trip is going to be absolutely rubbish at this rate!"

And then I grabbed my bag and stormed off. At that point I was so angry-upset I honestly thought I was going to walk all the way home, on my own! But I got to the front gate and wasn't sure which way to go. We've only become friends with Bella in the last few weeks and I've only been to her house a couple of times. Plus, Bella's mum was watching me from the window and Jess was talking to her, probably telling her all about my firepit calzone disaster and how her lavender bush got wrecked. So I knew I couldn't actually go any further. Instead I sat down with my back against the gate and wrote that shouty bit in my journal. Soon the girls appeared, and sat down either side of me, even though it was a bit of a squash.

"I'm fine by myself," I said grumpily, but of course they wouldn't go away.

"What's going on, Arch?" asked Shazmin, in a gentle voice. "Why is getting everything right for this trip with your dad so important to you?"

I shrugged. "I just want it to go really well, so we have fun together."

But that wasn't exactly true. There were loads of emotions bubbling up inside me – some that I hadn't even realized I was feeling before then. I knew I had to share them. After all, the whole point of the club is to find ways to help ourselves feel good, right? It had helped to talk about my feelings last time, when we were all in the hammock. So ... I had to make an effort.

It was really hard to put into words and when I tried, at first only a big sigh came out. But I tried again and soon I found myself saying, "I feel like everything has to go really, really well now in the practice or..."

I was quiet for ages. "Or what?" asked Bella gently.

"Or ... the whole trip will be ruined," I mumbled. "I know it's silly, but I really want it all to be perfect for my dad, so we have a great time together, but I can't seem to get anything right."

"Planning a brilliant surprise for your dad and wanting it to go well is natural," Bella said then. "But you can't control everything that happens. Now or on the actual trip."

"And even if it's not perfect you know it will still be amazing, don't you?" added Shazmin.

I shrugged again. (I'm getting good at that!) "Maybe," I muttered. But I still didn't feel like it would be amazing. Not if I couldn't get everything right.

"Come on," said Shazmin. "Let's go and have another try at that tent. *Together*, this time. But you can be in charge and I'll let you boss me about, just this once."

Well, I still felt a bit downcast, but that was an offer I couldn't refuse! So I got up and went round to the back garden with them. We did the tent OK that time, and Bella's mum came out with popcorn for us. Jess obviously *had* told her about my mishap because Kate brought out more calzone dough and filling too, so I could have another go at it. By then I wasn't thinking of it as such a *disaster* – thanks to my friends being so kind to me. Also, I said sorry about the lavender bush and luckily she just laughed about it and didn't look one bit annoyed – phew!

"You OK now, Archie?" Jess asked me quietly, while we were cooking the second calzone.

"Yes, thanks," I said, and I really, really was. I get that it's not about things being perfect, and I know that me and Dad will have a good time even if there are a few slip-ups. Obviously it will be great if we *DON'T* set our dinner on fire, though, *LOL!*

Oh, hang on – the movie the girls were watching on the iPad (the second one they've watched tonight!) has just ended and it's past ten and properly dark. It's time to pay back their kindness to me and put into action my brilliant plans to help them cure their fears of spookiness and spiders... They're going to be thanking me SO much after this!

Day of the Week: Sunday

Feelings I experienced today:

Sunday afternoon, 2.17 p.m., relaxing in my room.

I'm just looking to see where I got up to in the story of the practice camp out... Oh yeah – I remember now. So the movie ended and we all popped into the house to go to the loo. (I'll leave the going in a bush until the *actual* wild camping trip!) Then we got back in the tent, and snuggled down inside our sleeping bags, and I secretly got ready to help my friends with their fears. They say the best thing to do is face fears, isn't it? Get it over with. So that's what I was planning... Bella and Shazmin seemed to have forgotten about my plans, which was great, because I was sure they'd work far better if they were a complete surprise.

We turned our torches off but left the fairy lights on. Bella was still looking very nervous. "I don't think I can sleep out here," she said anxiously. Just then there was a tiny sound and she jumped. "Did you hear that? Maybe it was a fox or a badger ... or a burglar or a zombie?"

"How about I tell you a ghost story?" offered Shazmin. "That might help you relax."

Bella looked horrified. "How is a *ghost story* going to help me relax?!" she cried.

"OK, then," said Shazmin cheerfully. "I know, maybe Archie can tell you about the Higgs boron – again. That'll send you off to sleep in no time."

"Charming!" I huffed. "And it's the Higgs boson, actually. Or maybe Shazmin can tell you about all the different types of stage make-up – *again*. No, actually, we'd better not risk it – forget sleep, that might put you into a *coma*!"

Shazmin threw herself at me, still in her sleeping bag, and we had a kind of sleeping bag sumo wrestle. Bella joined in by throwing the sequinned cushions at us, and then leaping on top of the pile, totally squashing me.

It was really good fun, but then I remembered what I was supposed to be doing – helping my friends – and got back on the case. First I had to get Bella out of the tent and into the garden, so when we'd calmed down a bit I said, "Bel, could you show me where the cereal is, in case I get hungry in the night?"

"In the kitchen cupboard," she said, looking bemused. "I showed you earlier. Mum's leaving the door unlocked so we can get anything or come in if we want to."

"Yeah, but can you just show me again?" I asked, trying to look really confused and like I had forgotten in the last half an hour.

"Fine, OK," said Bella, and shuffled out of her sleeping bag. We crawled out of the tent and made our way across the garden, by the light of my torch. Halfway I stopped and said, "Oh no! I think I left my favourite jumper in the hammock. If I don't collect it, it'll get all damp. Can we just..."

"OK," said Bella. "But I'm sure it's in the tent, because—"

"It's not," I said quickly.

"All right, but stay close," she said. "You know I don't like the dark and all the spooky noises out here." With that she linked arms with me and we headed for the back of the garden, my torch lighting the way. When we were under the trees, where it was really dark, with loads of very helpful spooky noises, I said, "OK, Bella, remember the Listening in Nature. Just do the same now, but without the poem."

"Archie, what—?"

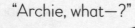

"Be brave, Bella, I know you can do it!" I said, and with that I turned and bolted back down the garden.

"Archie, don't leave me alone down here!" she shrieked. "I haven't got a torch!"

"I'm doing it to help you!" I called. "You'll be fine. You'll thank me later!"

I hurried back to the tent to put my Shazmin plan into action.

Shaz had her headphones on, and was busy drawing, which was perfect for my creepy crawlies fear-busting plan. I delved into my bag and pulled out a plastic tub containing the nine spiders I'd collected in the afternoon. With a flourish, I pulled off the lid and emptied them on to her drawing book. Of course she absolutely screamed the tent down at first. It was a bit worse than I'd imagined, even for Shazmin, but I kept on with my plan. "Breathe, Shazmin," I told her, in a really calm voice. "Breathe and release your fears..."

ARRGGHH!

I took a deep breath to demonstrate, but she just screamed again and flipped the drawing book into the air, sending the spiders flying across the tent as if they'd been shot out of tiny cannons. At that moment, Bella burst through the tent flaps, with leaves in her hair and a look of terror on her face.

"*ARCHIEEEEEEEE!*" they both *YELLED* at me. That's when I realized that my fear-facing plans hadn't worked as well as I'd hoped. Whoops!

They were really mad at me! They thought I was just playing horrible tricks on them. Of course, I did explain I was trying to help and they did eventually understand that, but they still marched off to the house, saying there was no way they could sleep in the tent after that. So those plans were a total FAIL and I was the only one left camping out last night. Well, Jess pitched her bivouac and slept beside the tent so I wouldn't be totally alone, but it doesn't really count. Being in the tent was really good, though, and I did actually get a good night's sleep.

SO ... analyzing the camping practice as a whole, I conclude that it was a success. We had fun this morning cooking sausages (and veggie sausages for Bella). Shazmin and Bella have just about forgiven me for the spooky noises and spider incidents! It's a shame that they didn't quite manage to conquer their fears, and maybe it wasn't the best way to go about things, thinking

about it! They certainly don't want any more help from me, they made that very clear!

I can't wait for the wild camping trip! I'm feeling really excited about it again – it will get Dad away from the stresses of home and we'll have some time together at last. I can put the tent up now, and I worked out why the first calzone fell into the fire, so that shouldn't happen again – the second one worked really well. Also, I've looked up some common bird calls – there's an amazing app I downloaded on Dad's phone where you can sing them and it identifies them for you and gives you loads of facts about the different birds. I've also brushed up on my stargazing info, so I know what's what and where's where, and I have a few great facts to share with Dad on that front too.

Roll on, next weekend!

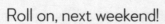

Day of the Week: _Monday_

Feelings I experienced today:

Monday after school, 4.22 p.m., writing this lying in the garden.

Only six days until the camping trip. I love doing all the secret planning! Jess is lending me the tent that me, Bella and Shazmin slept out in (well, only _I_ slept out in it in the end!) and bedrolls, a camping stove and all that stuff. We're making the calzone dough on Wednesday round at Bella's house then freezing it, so it's ready for me to take on Saturday. On Friday, Shazmin's going to bring me all the other ingredients for them and for breakfast on Sunday.

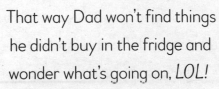

That way Dad won't find things he didn't buy in the fridge and wonder what's going on, _LOL!_

107

I've given her some of my savings (£8.48 to be precise!) and a list, and she's going shopping with her mum to get the stuff.

Jess has helped me find a wild camping place that's not too far away but far enough to feel like an adventure – it's on her friend from uni's parents' land, and she's stayed there before. There's a wood and a stream and a huge field. She showed me some pictures on her phone, when we were cooking our sausages on Sunday. It looks brilliant – properly wild, like, no toilets or table tennis, but not scary we-might-die-out-there wild, *LOL!*

Uncle James is coming round at ten o'clock on Saturday morning to stay here with Ed and Amos – he said no to having them in his flat again. He's only

just redecorated it after
the flying ketchup and
permanent marker incidents
that happened on his expensive
wallpaper when they visited before.
Speaking of my little brothers being a bit of a
nightmare, they're acting up and fighting with
each other even more than usual at the moment.
Dad says it's because it's so light in the evenings
and mornings at this time of year. They aren't
getting to sleep as easily and they're waking up
too early – so they're cranky and tired! Whatever
it is, it's stressing Dad out even more than usual
– and he's got a big work deadline this week. I'm
pretty glad I've got loads more years of being a
kid left before I have to grow up and deal
with all that kind of stuff! And it makes
me even happier about our official
Feeling Good Club plan – Dad's going to
need this surprise camping trip more than ever!

I've got to go and do my homework now, which is English. Oh, and I gave my poem in for the Home Achievements board and Ms Adeyemi loved it! Top grades, here I come!

Day of the Week: Tuesday

Feelings I experienced today:

Tuesday, 5.37 p.m., chilling out in the garden after playing a ton of games with Ed and Amos.

Only five days to go until the wild camp out! I really wished I could tell Mum about it today on Zoom but I couldn't risk Dad hearing! At lunchtime me, Shazmin and Bella walked all the way round the field while we went through the details of my plan.

"This is going to work just as well as the baking demo plan!" cried Shazmin, doing a twirl. "Which led to Bella acing her class talk, and to all of us getting to sign up for the show-in-a-week together. Which is really soon, by the way. Oh, I can't wait for the summer holidays!"

111

Show in a week!

Show-in-a-week is this drama thing at the arts centre, like a holiday club where you get given your parts and scripts for a show on the Monday, and then rehearse until Thursday. Then on Friday morning you do a full dress rehearsal with proper lights and sound and everything, and in the afternoon there's a performance for your friends and family. It's really brilliant fun – me and Shaz did it last year. It's going to be even better with Bella there this time!

"I can't wait either!" said Bella, her eyes gleaming. "There's the show-in-a-week, which I'm only a tiny bit terrified about, *LOL!* And now we've got the Feeling Good Club, we can have so much fun this summer! Plus, Rosh is coming to stay with us for at least a week. I can't wait to show her what we've done with the summerhouse – she's going to be blown away!"

"How are things between you guys now?" I asked as I jogged over to pick up a stray ball and chuck it back on to the basketball court.

"Great, thanks to you two helping me share my feelings with her," said Bella. "We managed to Zoom a couple of times last week too, even with all the homework she has, and our activities and things. And we even watched a movie together – we started it at exactly the same time. And we had the same pizza as each other!"

"That sounds so much fun!" said Shazmin. "We should do that one night even though we live close to each other!"

"We could have a movie in our clubhouse soon," I suggested, "with popcorn!"

It was so good, just chatting about stuff until the bell went. I'm so, so lucky to have such great friends! I'm not happy that Bella's best friend moved away, obviously – but it *is* great that she chose to start hanging around with me and Shazmin!

And, of course, it's *SO* exciting about the wild camping trip – I just can't wait! Oh, Dad's calling us in for dinner...

Day of the Week: Wednesday

Feelings I experienced today:

Wednesday at stupid 4.48 p.m. In my room. Everything is RUBBISH!

It's probably about 8,000 days to go until I get to camp out with Dad, because Uncle James has come down with flu and can't look after Ed and Amos. I found out this morning (he called and pretended he needed to talk to me about my gran's birthday) and I felt sick all the way to school. I walked really, really slowly, dragging my feet, and I had to keep stopping and blinking a lot because I felt like I was going to cry. Dad asked me what was wrong but I just mumbled that I had hay fever and then I started playing kick the stone with Ed and Amos so he wouldn't say anything else about it.

Yucky feeling

Bella and Shazmin were already in our classroom when I got in and they knew right away that something was wrong. We had to wait until break time to talk, but as soon as we got out on to the field I told them about Uncle James.

"Oh no, I'm so sorry, Arch," said Shazmin. "But can't you just do it in a couple of weeks' time?"

"No," I said wearily. "Uncle James will be off back to New York by then. He only lives here some of the time."

"Isn't there anyone else who could look after the twins?" asked Shazmin.

"No," I said flatly. "Even having a babysitter for the evening has always been a bit of a disaster – the ones we've had all made excuses not to come back!"

"Oh," said Shazmin. "I was going to suggest maybe Charita could come over, but I guess your dad won't agree to that."

"Definitely not, no." I felt too sad and upset to say more. We walked around in silence for a while. Then Bella said, "I know this trip was really important to you, Archie, I get that. But it seems to me that even more important is telling your dad how you feel about things at home. Tell him what you told us, about how you wish you had more time together, just the two of you, and feeling that your brothers and work take all his attention. If you just let him know how you're feeling, well, I know you can't do the trip, but

117

maybe there are other things you *can* do."

"Bella's right," said Shazmin. "There must be loads of other fun things you can do together instead ... at home ... with your brothers there."
I pulled a face and she trailed off, looking sheepish, then mumbled, "Or maybe not. But you should still tell him how you're feeling. Just so he knows."

I didn't say anything for ages. My chest felt funny even thinking about telling Dad my feelings. Like I said before, we don't really talk like that to each other. I was surprised the other day when he told me what he was like at my age, and how he struggled with finding people to hang around with when he was at junior school. I suppose it was nice that he shared, but that doesn't mean I'm going to share *my* feelings. Just thinking about it again now makes my heart bang and my mouth go dry.

And I don't want to seem like I'm complaining – Dad's got a lot on his plate at the moment, I get that.

Finally I said to my friends, "I know why you're saying I should tell Dad how I feel. You think it will make things better. But he's got so much going on at the moment, I don't want to give him something else to worry about."

"I'm sure he'd rather know," Shazmin insisted.

"I'm sure he wouldn't," I countered. Why was she questioning me? I know my own dad, right? "I mean, what's the point?" I went on, maybe a bit grumpily. "It'll just make him feel bad, but there isn't anything he can do about it, is there?"

The girls exchanged glances, but they didn't say anything else about it. I know there's loads of stuff about how good it is to share your feelings in the handout from Kris, and we have the whole club and everything. But actually, sometimes, I really think it's better to keep stuff to yourself, so you don't upset people or worry them. And this is *definitely* one of those times.

I managed to forget about things a bit during science because we were doing the history of astronomy and I had to correct Mr Lacey a couple of times when the worksheets he'd probably just downloaded from the internet weren't quite correct on some facts. But mainly I just felt totally awful all day. All that prep and all that planning and all that hard work... And Shazmin and her mum had already been to the shops for me, so I'd also spent £8.48 of my savings on basically vegetables.

Argh, I'm feeling really upset again writing all this down. I won't be getting my special time with Dad, nothing will change at home, and Mum's away for over two more months. I suppose we'll just have to go camping then, when she's back, but that seems like absolutely *forever* away. And the place we're going is all arranged...

My friends were totally out of ideas for how to save the trip today, and so am I. So I guess it's definitely, one hundred per cent cancelled. And I should probably just stop thinking about it, because it's totally pointless. But it's the only thing in my mind and I feel so disappointed!

CANCELLED!

Wednesday, 8.57 p.m., in my room at bedtime.
Well, actually, it's after bedtime, but I just quickly
wanted to write in here what happened tonight.
Dad must have noticed how totally miserable I was
at teatime because he came up to my room to
check on me when I was doing my reading, saying,
"Are you OK, Arch? You seem a bit down."

I shrugged. "Guyeeeah," I said, which wasn't
exactly lying, but I couldn't tell him the truth –
either about the cancelled camping trip or about
feeling we don't spend much time together any
more. Well, I *thought* I couldn't. But Dad came
in and sat down on my desk chair and kind of
swivelled one way and then the other, like someone
who isn't going to take "guyeeeah" for an answer.

"What is it, Arch?" he said then. I did want to
talk to him, and I was trying to find the words to
begin when his phone beeped and he got it out and

122

glanced at it. "I'll just ... deal with ... this..." he said, while typing a quick reply. Then he looked at me expectantly.

"Well, I—" I began, not really knowing what the next words would be.

Then his phone beeped again and he started reading something else. Suddenly another angry-upset volcano erupted in me, a really explosive one, like one with magma that had loads of big carbon dioxide and water vapour bubbles in it. I found myself yelling, "Dad! We were talking! Even when you come to talk to me you're not actually properly *here*!"

Molten lava explosion or what?! Wow, where did that come from?! That's the third time now! He looked up sharply, blinked at me like he was waking up from a dream and put the phone away. Like, actually *away* in his back pocket.

"Sorry, Arch," he said then. "I've got a really complicated job on at the moment. With so many demands from the client, I feel like Edward Witten trying to wrestle all the superstring theories into a single theory in eleven dimensions – but I bet this is harder!"

I didn't smile or laugh. I didn't feel like joking things away, even though I'm usually the one to do that if someone's worried or upset. Instead, all the anger went out of me and I started to cry. "I'm serious," I said, through the tears. "You're always on your phone. Why can't we just talk, just us, with nothing getting in the way?"

Dad looked really upset then. "Oh, Archie, I'm so sorry," he said. "Me being so busy is no excuse.

I should be giving you my full attention. I'm really, really sorry." Dad suddenly getting all serious like that and saying sorry made it easier for me to share more of my feelings somehow.

"It's just, we never get to spend any time together any more," I mumbled. "You're always busy with work, or Ed and Amos, or cooking, cleaning, washing, all that stuff..."

He sighed. "I don't *enjoy* having to do everything by myself, you know," he said. "But you're right, that shouldn't mean that we don't get quality time together."

He looked so exhausted and sad that I felt really sorry for him. I lay on my bed and put my feet up on his legs on the swivel chair. "Ewww, change your socks!" he joked, but he didn't move, and I didn't either.

I knew I should say the rest of how I was feeling then. I closed my eyes. It was easier to talk like that, somehow. "I've been feeling like you don't have much time to spend with me," I said.

"Archie—" Dad began, but I carried on. Now I'd started, I wanted to say everything. "So me, Bella and Shazmin came up with this plan, for you and me to go wild camping on our own. We actually camped out in her garden at the weekend, not in the clubhouse. It was a practice, so I could learn loads of cool things that we could do together, like hollowing out a dead camel and fire lighting, and making firepit calzones, and identifying animal tracks, and putting up the tent."

"Archie, that's amazing!" said Dad. "Well, you know, apart from the camel thing."

"It would have been amazing," I replied. "I secretly arranged for Uncle James to look after Ed and Amos, but, well, you know he's got flu now, so the trip's off."

Dad lifted up my legs and came and lay on the bed next to me, and together we both looked up at the twinkling cosmos on my ceiling.

"We were meant to be sleeping out together under the actual stars," I said quietly. "Spending time, hanging out. That was the plan."

"It was a great plan," said Dad, "and I would have loved it. But you're right about your brothers – I can't really rely on anyone else to look after them. I think we'll just have to hold on until your mum gets home in September."

"It won't be summer by then," I grumped.

"It can still be really warm, though," said Dad. He shifted and looked at me. "By the way, what exactly *was* that about a dead camel?"

I couldn't help smiling then. "Nothing. Just something I saw on TV, for if you don't have a tent."

"And a tent is…"
Dad's eyes twinkled.

"For if you don't have a dead camel,"
we both said together.

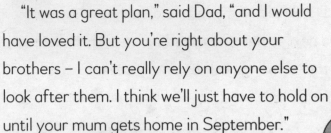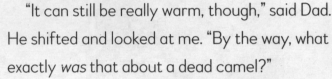

Dad sat up and I did too. "I'm really sorry, Archie. And I wish you'd told me sooner about how you've been feeling. But please know that I

would absolutely love to spend more time with you, and the minute things ease up a bit we can make some plans. And even before then, there are things I will find time for, to do together at home."

I couldn't help smiling a bit. "Like fill up the bathtub with homemade slime or make our own volcanoes with fizzy drinks and sweets?"

Dad laughed. "Maybe." He ruffled my hair. "OK, time for bed. And thanks, Archie – thanks for being you."

"You're welcome," I said, with a grin. "And I'll take that as a definite yes on the slime and sweet volcanoes."

"A definite maybe," said Dad, beaming at me.

So ... I shared how I felt, and Dad got it! I feel so much better, I kind of wonder why I didn't just say something before, like the girls suggested, *LOL!* But it's always harder to imagine doing tricky things before you do them, and afterwards you just think, *Phew! I did it!* Obviously I'm still disappointed about the camping trip, but it's amazing how much better I feel!

Day of the Week: Thursday

Feelings I experienced today:

Thursday, 4.04 p.m., out on the swing in the garden.

It's been such an awesome day! I'll go back and write the full story in here, from the beginning – but I'll have to write quickly, because my dad's taking me round to Bella's soon for our Feeling Good Club meeting! Bella has Swimming Club after school (she's really good!) so we're waiting until she's home before we go round.

So, this morning I couldn't wait to get to school and tell Bella and Shazmin all about the chat I had with Dad and how great it was and how much better I felt. I told them in the book corner before registration and they were so happy for me that I ended up in one of Shazmin's squealy hug things

and Bella joined in
and Mr Lacey had
to tell us to quieten
down a bit!

"The camping trip's still off,
though, right?" asked Shazmin as we sat down in
our places and got out our reading books.

"Yep," I said, feeling a pang of sadness in my
stomach.

"Hmm, we'll have to have a think about that,"
she said.

"Yes, we will," said Bella.

They must have worked something out during
humanities, when they were looking things up
in the book corner together, because at break
time they were acting very, very mysterious and
very, very pleased with themselves. I'd hardly had
a chance to get my cereal bar out of my bag
before they linked arms with me – one on each
side – and marched me out into the playground.

"Hey, what's going on?" I asked, trying to get my arm up to my mouth, and then when that didn't work, trying to get my mouth down to my arm.

"We have a brilliant idea to make everything OK," said Shazmin. And with that she lunged at my cereal bar and bit off a massive chunk.

"Right, that's it!" I said, wriggling my arms out from their grip and whipping the rest away from her. "No more marching me around. I won't move until you tell me what you're up to."

"Not until we get to the eco hut," said Shazmin, after she'd finished her huge mouthful of MY cereal bar! "Come on, quick, or those Year Sixes will get it first."

Bella held out her packet of mini rice cakes. "Have some of these, Arch," she said. "And come

133

with us. Trust me, you'll like this."

The eco hut is at the far end of the field. Luckily it was empty, so we went in and sat down on the benches. Bella was grinning at me, and Shazmin looked very, very pleased with herself.

"What's this brilliant idea then?" I asked them.

"It's about your camping trip," said Shazmin.

I sighed. "There *is* no camping trip, you know that. Unless you've found a way to travel back in time and make my little brothers not exist."

"We're working on that," said Bella. "But meanwhile..."

"May we present..."

"Dun-dun-duuuh..."

"The Camping Trip Is BACK ON Plan!"

Well, I was really listening then! "But how?"
I asked.

Shazmin beamed at me. "Well, of course it's
great that you talked to your dad, but it's not
great that the camping trip is still off. So, we
thought really hard in the book corner and we
turned the whole thing round and round trying to
work out how to make it happen."

"And we turned it round and round so much we
turned it on its head and realized the answer," said
Bella. "Your brothers *should* go with you!"

My heart sank – I'd really thought they might
have an *actual* solution until that point! "Thanks
so much for trying," I said, with a sigh. "But that's
never going to work. Dad will be more stressed
than ever trying to stop Ed and Amos getting
into danger or trying to keep them entertained

without screens. And he'll have zero time for me."

"That's where *we* come in," said Bella. "We're going to come with you too, and be on full-time Ed and Amos duty to keep them safe and occupied..."

"So you still get to have loads of one-on-one time with your dad," said Shazmin. She grinned at me and added, "You're welcome."

Well, I was completely surprised by that – I couldn't say anything for ages, my brain was whirring so fast.

"You've got a big people-carrier," said Bella. "So we can all fit in the car, even with the camping stuff."

I nodded. I hadn't been thinking about room in the car, though. OK, so it wouldn't be the same, but if I went with the girls' plan, me and Dad could still go... Then I remembered something.

"Hang on, didn't you two absolutely swear you're never going to camp out ever again? Like, EVER?" I asked.

Bella started to look a bit nervous at that point, and began swinging her legs back and forth, scuffing her shoes on the dirt floor. "Yes, we did," she said. "But we have decided to try to face our fears and do it, because we really want to help you."

"Because you're such a great friend," added Shazmin, "who always shares his cereal bars with us…"

I couldn't help smiling then. "Well, I didn't exactly get a choice about that, did I?" I said. And I made up my mind. "Thanks so much, you two," I said. "Yes, please! Let's do it! The camping trip is back on!"

We all had a big hug then and Shazmin did her happy dance, which made the Year 3s who'd been spying on us through the window run off giggling.

"Huh, me and Rosh used to spy on the big kids in the eco hut!" said Bella, laughing.

"Now we *are* the big kids," I said. "When did that happen?"

I felt so much appreciation for my friends then. I'm still amazed (and grateful) they'd do this for me, when they're both scared of camping out, for different spidery or spooky reasons!

"So, are you going to tell your dad about the trip?" Shazmin asked. "Or is it staying as a surprise?"

"I actually told him about it when we talked last night," I said. "But obviously he thinks it's off now. So I could still make it a surprise if I don't say it's back on. But, you know what, I don't want it to be one any more. I'm too excited! I'm going to tell him the second I see him!"

"All sorted then!" said Shazmin. "Go, team!"

"*Almost* all sorted," said Bella. "Now me and you have to get to work on our fears, Shaz,

because once we're camping out in the wild, there
will be no chance to run screaming back into the
house like last time!"

"I can help you again—" I began, but before I
could say any more, they both cried, "No, no, no!"
and, "No way!"

"We have a brilliant plan to bust our fears too,"
said Bella.

"Wow, you *were* busy in that book corner,"
I joked. "Did you actually do any work at all in that
lesson?"

The girls giggled. "Not really," said Shazmin.

"Anyway," said Bella, "our plan definitely does
NOT involve getting left down at the bottom of
the garden in the dark!"

"Or being showered in spiders!" added
Shazmin, with a shudder.

I winced. "Sorry. Although technically I threw
them on your drawing book."

"No worries, mate," said Shazmin, in an

Australian accent. "We've found something in the handout from Kris that's going to actually help us." She grinned at Bella. "And we can do it at our Feeling Good Club meeting after school!"

"You've got it all worked out!" I laughed. "You've organized my entire life and thought of everything. Anything else I should know?"

Bella laughed too. "Yep, ghost stories are one hundred per cent banned from the camp out!" she said. "I'm going to face my fear of spooky noises and go for it, but I definitely don't need anything making it worse!"

"Deal!" I said. Then with a grin, I added, "It was a dark, dark night..."

"Stop it!" shrieked Bella. "Not even now in the daylight, OK?!"

"Whooooooo!" went Shazmin. "I'm a scary ghost!"

Whooooooooo!

And with that we all tumbled outside on to the field, laughing. The camping trip is back on and I feel even better than before, like probably just as amazing as Einstein when he came up with his theory of general relativity ... and his theory of special relativity, for that matter!

So, as soon as we got out of school, I told Dad Bella and Shazmin's idea about the wild camping – that we would all go, my brothers and them too. He was so happy! I made him promise to leave all the arrangements to us, and he says he will. But he did insist on calling Steve and Keerti, just to check it really was OK for Bella and Shazmin to come with us. And, of course, there was a big yes from both of them! I'm so, so, so, so, so, so, so super excited! Oh, gotta go – Dad says it's time to go to Bella's – hooray!

Still Thursday, 7.42 p.m., back home after going to Bella's.

I'm trying to write this at the kitchen table, while having to pretend to be an alien at the same time and getting blasted with foam pellets from Ed's laser blaster. It's made out of cereal boxes and tape, and I helped him construct it, BTW, because I was so cheered up still when I got back. Jess dropped me home – it must be so handy for Bella to have an older sister who can drive!

So, anyway, I wanted to write about the Feeling Good Club meeting we had at Bella's. Our clubhouse is just so brilliant and it looks amazing now! Steve borrowed a stepladder from their next-door neighbours, and Jess finished off painting the stripes. Steve has run a power cable out there so we can have proper lights and heating in the winter – and my projector of stars on the ceiling all year round! I took it with me today and it looks absolutely brilliant! We got to have a picnic tea in there too, all together, because Bella was so hungry after swimming she couldn't wait. It was great fun having sandwiches and grapes and apple slices and crisps and squash and everything in our very own clubhouse.

Of course, I made the girls say the secret password as they went in, *LOL*, and we put on our club badges – and then we stopped to have our feast! Once everything was eaten, Shazmin stood up and did a twirl on the wooden floorboards. "OK, I call this meeting of the Feeling Good Club officially to order," she announced. "Bella, over to you."

"So, we're going to do the Breathing Magic mindfulness activity," Bella said. I flicked to that page in my handout and had a quick read. "Sorry, girls, but I don't think this is going to help you with your spooky and spidery fears," I said. "It's just breathing in and out – how is that going to do anything?"

"It's magic, Archie," said Bella. "Look, as you breathe in you say, 'I breathe in calm', and as you breathe out, you say, 'I breathe out worries'. You're actually getting the worries to *go out* of you!"

I wished I had as much confidence in the magic of mindfulness as Bella did! Shazmin obviously did, though, because she said, "And see, it says here that we can also make up our own words, like our own personal magic spells!"

To be fair, making up our own personal magic spells with the power to banish our worries and fears did sound pretty cool. The handout said to begin by thinking about how we usually feel in our bodies and minds when we're worried and upset.

"When I'm upset, my stomach starts churning," said Shazmin. "And I feel frustrated and like shouting and crying, all at the same time. Oh, I'm getting it *right now*! Look! I feel like that even *thinking* of Charita helping herself to my ring light that I saved up my own money for and then breaking it and not even really saying sorry properly."

Bella looked at me. "I..."
I began, but then nothing else would come out of my mouth.

"You can just write it in your journal, if you like," she said. "It doesn't say on the sheet that you have to share out loud."

"Thanks, but it's OK," I said, determined to join

in and share my feelings. "I feel so upset about Ed and Amos getting all the attention at home," I told them. "And then I feel bad for feeling that, like I'm a bad big brother. I want to do more nice things with them, but I just seem to end up moaning about their mess and telling them to go away a lot! So I guess I feel irritated in my mind and just want to get away from them. And in my body I feel frustrated, like I need to go running really fast but I can't." I paused and took a deep breath. Again, just like with Dad, it was a big relief to say how I felt. "I hadn't realized that my upset was ruining the fun we could be having together," I said then. "I'd just never thought of it like that."

"It's funny how you often don't realize things until you say them out loud, isn't it?" said Bella.

Letting worries out makes space for...

good feelings to come in!

"And how they can come *bursting* out of you, even though you're trying not to let them."

"Yeah, like magma out of a volcano," I agreed. "Like when I shouted at you guys." I went red. "Twice. And at Dad the other night."

Shazmin giggled and Bella's eyes widened. "Did you? That's very un-Archie!"

"Yep," I said. "My emotions erupted like Mount Vesuvius, which destroyed Pompeii in AD79. But on the upside it led to us having that great talk."

"Mine burst out when Rohisha moved," said Bella. "I ended up yelling at her on Zoom that she'd gone off to a new life and left me behind." She smiled shyly and added, "My heart was pounding and my head felt like it was going to explode. I was really upset then, that's for sure! Really stressed out! And when I'm worried, I feel sick, just really sick, and my mind won't stop going round and round thinking about the worry over and over again."

"I hate it when that happens," I said. I really know what she means too – when my mind gets hold of a worry, I can't seem to stop thinking about it!

"It must be so complicated, being you two," said Shazmin. "All those feelings swirling around inside you! When Charita takes my stuff I feel like shouting and crying all at once, and I just do it. And maybe try to kick her in the ankles. Then I feel better. And that's fair enough because she deserves it!"

"Shazmin!" I cried. "Do you really kick her?"

"I try," she said, "but she kind of holds my arms and we end up in a wrestly fight. But that's not going to help me beat my fear of creepy crawlies, is it? I can't wrestle a spider, can I? Do spiders even *have* ankles?"

We all laughed at that. It felt really good to talk about my feelings with my friends. I suppose I'd usually make a joke to avoid opening up about emotions, or change the subject on to something easier, like particle acceleration and the collision of lead ions, for example. Anyway, I was really looking forward to trying the Breathing Magic! We all settled down and got comfy, and focused on our breathing. "Breathing in, I breathe in calm," said Shazmin soothingly, which made all three of us burst into giggles, so instead we thought of the words in our heads as we breathed in and out.

I breathe in calm, I thought. And then, *I breathe out worries.* After a few minutes of that, we tried the other one. *I breathe in relaxation, I breathe out stress.*

I got so relaxed I had to lie down and Shazmin poked me with her foot to check I was still awake. I poked her back and we were all in a foot-poking fight for a while – whoops! But then we got back on the case – facing fears!

"Right, time to create our very own magic spells!" said Shazmin, pulling her journal towards her. We spent a few minutes writing our spells and then shared what we'd created.

"I breathe in peace, I breathe out spiders," said Shazmin, as she wrote. Then she said, "Oh no! That's a horrible image, breathing out spiders!" She scribbled it out in her journal. "OK, let's go for 'I breathe out fear'."

Bella shared hers. "I breathe in courage, I breathe out TERROR!" she said, which made us all laugh. "I might change that to 'fear', like yours," she added. "Saying 'terror' is making it worse, not better!"

I chose, 'I breathe in kindness, I breathe out

jealousy'. I don't want to be the sort of big bro who's jealous of his little brothers getting his dad's attention. Kindness seemed like the best word to describe the way I want to be with them – just, like, nice and patient and not annoyed all the time!

So we became very still again and breathed in and out, sometimes saying our words out loud and sometimes saying them in our heads. Our breathing got so we all matched up with each other and it really did feel like we were working magic! In the end we laid down and did it.

It's hard to explain exactly how brilliant it felt, but I'm definitely going to do it again, for anything else I want to breathe out and replace with something better, using whatever words I decide on. Like, if I'm feeling a bit awkward in the boys' changing rooms before P.E. when loads of people are messing around and I don't really know how to join in, I could do, *I breathe in confidence, I breathe out awkwardness.*

"How are we going to test whether it's worked?" I asked, when we'd all opened our eyes. "Shall I go and get some more spiders and we can—"

"No!" Shazmin shrieked. "I suppose we'll just have to find out at the camp out. I'll keep doing this whenever I remember until then, though!"

"Me too!" said Bella. "So there's no need to 'help' me either, OK, Arch? Promise?"

I laughed and held up my hands. "OK, I promise! I realize now I didn't have the world's *best* methods of helping you guys!"

After that, we wrote in our Feeling
Good Club journals about how we'd
found the Breathing Magic activity,
and Bella drew a picture of herself in
a big, starry cloak with a magic wand.
Above it she wrote in huge letters
I CHOOSE COURAGE. "I'm going to look
at that whenever I remember to," she told
us, "and draw a bigger version to stick on the wall
in my room. I'm going to do that Breathing Magic
loads and loads. Like when I'm bored in science,
for example!"

"How could you ever be bored in science?" I
gasped, and accidentally on purpose knocked her
off her cushion. Then we had a kind of cushion
fight that morphed into us trying to acrobatically
balance each other on our feet, like we were
flying, and then that was it – time to go home!

Bella's mum gave me the frozen calzone dough

they'd made me and I managed to hide it in the freezer without Dad noticing! Even though he knows about the camping trip now, I still want to surprise him with all the details.

So after a second tea at home of waffles and beans (just breathing made me very hungry obviously, *LOL!*), Ed and Amos were pestering me to help them make sonic blaster anti-alien guns for their game. For a change I didn't say "no" really grumpily and escape up to my room. Instead I gathered up some craft stuff and did it with them at the table here, and that's why I'm being pelted with foam pellets every time they run into the room.

So our Breathing Magic spells are working, I reckon – I already felt kinder and did something nice for them. Dad even noticed and thanked me when he popped out of his study to get a cup of tea just now, which felt really good. And he took some time to have a chat with me. Excitement

about the camping trip is bubbling up inside me,
like a volcano again, but a happy volcano instead
of an upset one!

And Dad's really excited too and looking
forward to getting away from all the stresses of
home. It will still be loads of fun, even with my
brothers there! I think I'll go and put on this alien
mask I've got in my room and hide somewhere
and spring out on the minions – hee hee hee!

Day of the Week: Saturday

Feelings I experienced today:

Saturday, 1.04 p.m.

We're off! I'm writing this in the car. I'm sitting in the front next to Dad while Shazmin and Bella are taming my brothers in the back – they've turned the seats round to make a four, like they're riding in a taxi. It was brilliant this morning – I went into Mum and Dad's room and jumped on Dad like when I was little and he groaned and went, "Get off, Archie, it's Saturday, I'm having a lie-in!"

"No, you're not," I said. "It's camping day! Time to get up!"

"But we're not going until after lunch!" he groaned.

"Exactly! Only six hours to go!" I cried, bouncing on him a bit more.

"Oh, all right, you're in charge!" he said, sitting up suddenly then pinning me down and tickling me.

I managed to get free and then raced back through the door to go and get my bros out of bed, shouting, "Camping, camping!"

It was the first they'd heard about the trip – we'd kept it a secret from them for fun (and to stop them getting too overexcited beforehand!). They went absolutely wild when I explained what we were doing, like they'd had ten packets of sweets each!

A bit later on I helped them pack their rucksacks and persuaded them to only bring three cuddly toys each.

"Brown bear has to come," said Ed, shoving his huge bear into his bag.

"Isn't he a bit big..." I began.

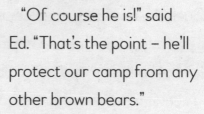

"Of course he is!" said Ed. "That's the point – he'll protect our camp from any other brown bears."

I laughed at that. "Oh, Ed, there won't be any brown bears where we're camping. It's not like we're taking a plane to Florida and going to the Everglades!"

"Best to be careful, though," said Amos, joining in, while putting a massive cuddly Tyrannosaurus rex into his bag!

"You know, the way to protect your camp from

158

bears is to mark your territory by weeing all the way round the edge of it," I told them. Well, there was loads of shrieking and laughing about that, of course, and they both insisted they're doing that when we're all set up, *LOL!*

Bella and Shazmin got here just after lunch, and we packed up the car with all the kit we borrowed from Jess (including two tents now!). It just got more and more and more exciting with everything we put in the car and then we put *ourselves* in the car and then we were off!

Ugh, I'm *feeling* a bit less excited now though and a bit sicker. Dad just said I should stop writing while we're driving because I look like I'm going to vomit, and I think that's probably a good...

BLEUGH!!!!!

Only joking, *LOL!* But OK, ugh, I will stop now.

Saturday afternoon. We're here, and it's amazing! I don't know the exact time. We've just put up the tents and I'm having a rest. We're camping in a field right by a wood – Jess's directions were perfect after the sat nav stopped knowing where we were. I'm writing short bits in this journal when I can because I don't want to forget anything.

The girls said a big no way to me doing a video diary on Dad's phone – well, I started one but then Shazmin slipped in the mud and fell flat on her face so she was full body covered in it, and she made me delete it and promise not to do any more! Luckily she's brought tons of changes of clothes – it's like she thinks we're at a posh hotel or something rather than out in the middle of nowhere, *LOL!*

It's absolutely amazing here, I love it! There's no one else around so we don't have to worry about Ed and Amos bothering anyone. They've just been running about, yelling and having stick fights, happy as anything. Putting the tents up went really well too – this time I remembered to peg them down! Dad was very impressed and I felt really proud of myself. Me and Dad did them together while Shazmin and Bella were playing in the field with the minions, and that was really nice.

"When did you learn how to do this, Arch?" Dad asked me as we knocked the ground pegs in with mallets.

"At Bella's," I said. "I learned tons of things so that we could have the best camp out ever."

"That's brilliant," said Dad. He stopped banging the tent peg he was on for a moment and turned to look at me. Really *look* at me. "This is absolutely amazing and I'm so honoured you've done it all for me," he said. "It really is great, Arch. I love it. Thank you."

Well, I felt a bit embarrassed then, and I was tempted to just mumble something and go on to the next tent peg, but instead I looked back properly at Dad and smiled and said, "I'm glad you like it. And thanks for saying all that."

"I love you so much, Archie," he said, and put down the mallet and jumped on me, yelling, "Man hug!" We had a funny, back

slapping sort of joke hug and
then a very, very real hug and
it was absolutely brilliant.

Oh, and changing the
subject, the Magic Breathing
must not have worked quite
yet, because Shazmin's
still terrified of creepy
crawlies, I can officially
report. I know this because
she was setting up our little
fold-out table and getting the food and drinks
out so we can cook later and an earwig ran over
her hand. She screamed and jumped around,
shaking it off. I don't know if Bella's still as
scared of spooky noises after the Magic
Breathing – I guess we'll find out

Yikes!

tonight. Oh, got to go, the girls
want me to join in something with
them...

Still Saturday. We've had our firepit calzones (yum!) and we're all just chilling out for a while now. I'm writing this sitting on a handy tree stump!

We actually really needed a chill-out, because it's been a very, very eventful few hours since I last wrote in here!

I'll pick up writing where I left off. That way I won't miss anything out. When the girls called me over, I put this journal down and went to join them. They both looked very pleased with themselves. Bella was holding Kris's handout of mindfulness activities. "We thought we'd try this on Ed and Amos," she said, turning the sheet so I could see it.

"Silly Walking and Silent Walking," I read. I glanced over to where my brothers were

wrestling around on the
ground, arguing with each
other. That quite often
happens when they've
played together for a
while – it goes a bit wrong!

"You started it!" yelled Amos. "I'm going to put
ten slugs on your head tonight, so there!"

"No, *you* started it, and I'm going to stick your
hand in warm water so you wee in your sleeping
bag, so there, there, there!"

"That doesn't work!" yelled Amos. "And now it's
going to be twenty slugs, so there!"

We all winced as they accidentally knocked
heads, and started arguing even more loudly.
"Ow! You did that on purpose!"

"No, *you* did!"

"No, *you* did! You know you did. No returns!"

"Just saying *no returns* doesn't mean I did it!"

"Good luck with the Silent Walking," I told my

friends, with a cheeky smile.

"We need to distract them from the ... THAT. Whatever it is they're doing," said Shazmin, wincing as Ed's knee connected with Amos's head. "Your dad's starting to look stressed and we want him to have a good time, don't we?"

She was right. By then, poor Dad was trying to separate my brothers and he had that look on his face like he just needed to lie down in a dark room for about twenty hours.

"Perhaps Silent Walking isn't the answer," said Bella. "Maybe we should start with the Silly Walking."

"I appreciate what you're trying to do," I said. "Really. But when those two get in a mood like this, no one can do anything about it. I don't see them joining in *any* walking, to be honest."

But Shazmin wasn't put off. Instead she just smiled and looked determined. "Ah, well, maybe no one *else* could do anything about it," she said,

"but you haven't seen me in action yet. Watch."
And with that, she sashayed over to them. Bella
and I followed close behind – we wanted to see
this!

"Stand back, I'll handle this," Shazmin told my
dad.

"Well, I—" he began, but he did stand back as
she dived in and pulled my bros apart.

"Right, you two, that's enough of that," she said
strictly. "We're doing something really cool now
and you'll want to join in."

"OK, that's impressive," said my dad.

"I don't take any nonsense!" said Shazmin,
looking pleased with herself.

But then Ed wiped his runny nose on the back
of his hand and narrowed his eyes at Amos. "I'm
not doing anything with *him*," he said.

"Yes, you are," said Shazmin, still confident.
"Look."

She smiled at my dad and said, "Time to bring

out the big guns." She went over to her bag and pulled out a box of these really delicious Indian sweets that her parents had given her to bring.

She held them up to show Dad, to make sure my brothers could have them.

"Excellent move," he said.

"You'll get some of these, but only if you work together in the Silly Walking we're going to do," she told Ed and Amos. "It's not a competition – well, the *competition* is how perfectly in sync your silly walks are."

My brothers looked a bit confused about that and so did I, probably! But they wanted the sweets, so they didn't argue.

In no time at all us three and my bros were all doing the Mindful Walking, starting with Silly Walking, while Dad watched, smiling. Sneaky Shazmin even got my bros to quieten down and focus before we started, by telling them there was a dragon in their bellies. Yes, really! She said we needed to breathe deeply into our tummies so that our dragons could wake up and come and play with us, and give us lots of great ideas for silly walks. I think she might be a genius!

Well, Amos sat down, closed his eyes and started to breathe deeply when Shazmin did. But Ed just scuffed at the ground with his trainer and said it was boring... Until Amos said, "Shazmin, it's happening! My dragon's waking up!"

"Huh! That's not fair! I want a dragon too!" cried Ed.

"Then you know what you've got to do," said Shazmin, with a twinkle in her eye.

So Ed sat down right next to Amos and started the deep breathing. Soon he was calling out,  "Shazmin, Shazmin, my dragon's waking up too!

And it's way, way better than *his* one."

"My one's going to breathe fire on your one and toast his bum off!" Amos replied.

"Right, time for the Silly Walking," said Shazmin, in a business-like way, before they could start arguing again. "Up you get!"

Then she started guiding them. "It says here to take the silliness up in stages," she said.

"Looking at them that's probably a good idea!" said Bella. My brothers were walking in loads of silly ways, hopping and leaping and looking like robots, but they were also trying to grab each other's legs to make the other one fall over.

"So we're going to start off by just walking like ourselves," said Shazmin confidently, and they stopped and turned to listen to her – miracle! We all tried it and it turned out to be much harder that you'd imagine – just walking normally like yourself feels really strange when you actually think about it.

We brought
up the silliness
level and we had
amazing fun walking
in the silliest ways
we could think of.
We were all in stitches
by the time we got up
to ten, Top Level Silliness! We did one final lap of
the field walking in as silly a way as we could and
then collapsed in a giggling heap. Ed hugged me
and I hugged him back, and it was really nice.

Dad waved me over then, as he wanted me
to show him how to get the gas stove going, so
he could have his coffee. Shazmin said, "You go,
Arch, we can look after these two. We'll play
some games with them over by the woods."

"Yeah, and I can be a bear!" said Amos. "Grrr!"

"I can be a lion and eat you!" said Ed.

"Lions can't eat bears – I'll pounce on you and

attack you with my claws!" cried Amos.

"Off we go, being bears and lions!" said Shazmin, with a big roar. I must have looked a bit worried because she said, "Honestly, Archie, we'll be fine! Won't we, Bella?"

"Yep," said Bella. "We'll just stay here in the field, where you can see us."

"Go and have some time with your dad," said Shazmin breezily. "We're having fun, aren't we, guys? Yeah!" And with that she high-fived Ed and Amos, and chased them round and round, with Bella following behind.

"Thanks, Shaz," I said. Then I went back to the tent and sat on one of the camping chairs next to Dad and soon we got really involved in talking.

I made Dad a second cup of coffee on the camping stove and he even let me connect up the new gas bottle and light it and pour out the boiling water. It was so brilliant, just the two of us, and he didn't look at his phone once. We talked properly about wormholes and time travel for ages with no distractions. Shazmin and Bella were doing a great job of keeping Ed and Amos entertained with one game after another, and the girls looked like they were enjoying it as much as my bros.

"We should see if those guys want a drink, or a snack," said Dad, opening a bag of popcorn and munching a handful. "They're probably ready for a break."

"Oh, I'm sure they're fine," I said, not wanting

my one-on-one time with Dad to end. "If they want something, they'll come back up here."

Dad sat back in his chair and stretched his legs out in front of him. "I guess you're right. The minions certainly seem to be enjoying themselves."

Soon, though, they did all troop up to us and I poured out some orange squash from the ready-made-up bottles we'd brought with us, while Dad tipped some popcorn into Jess's bamboo picnic bowls for each of us. Then I suggested we make a start on building the fire, so when it became dusk we could all sit around it and toast marshmallows and stuff.

"We can collect some wood from the forest," Amos suggested.

Dad laughed and opened the boot of the car. "I've got some here – dry and ready to go, thanks to Jess and you guys." He gave me and the girls a beaming smile.

"Aaaaaaw, but getting real firewood is way better," whined Ed. "We could chop down a tree and then—"

"There will be no chopping down trees," said Dad sternly. He didn't take them seriously, and neither did we, but maybe we should have done ... because of what happened next. Me, Dad and the girls got involved with building the fire – clearing a space and then making a ring of stones before stacking up kindling and logs in the centre. One minute Ed and Amos were there, helping us, and the next – poof! – they'd vanished.

At first we didn't panic – we just thought they were hiding in the tents or behind the car, but when we couldn't see them anywhere obvious we all started to worry.

"They're not in the field," called Shazmin as she jogged back up to the tents after checking every corner.

"Or up the lane," said Bella as she reappeared

round the bend that led to our little camping spot.

Suddenly Dad looked horrified. "Oh no," he groaned. "I bet they've gone off into the woods. Remember – they wanted to collect firewood and chop down a tree?"

Even as he was still speaking, we started running down the field to the woods.

"Ed! Amos!" Dad called. "Come out here immediately!" No reply. "They could have got themselves lost by now," he said as we reached the trees. He looked really stressed. "I've no idea how big this wood is! We'd better split up to search. You three go that way. I'll go this way. Stay together, OK?" And with that he dashed off into the trees, shouting, "Ed! Amos! Come here right now!"

Bella turned to me, looking panicked. Shazmin didn't look much better. "Oh my goodness, Archie, what are we going to do?" she cried. "They could be anywhere..."

"OK, OK, calm down, breathe," I told her, even though I didn't feel very calm myself. Bella started slow, deep breathing into her belly, like we'd done with Ed and Amos when we were pretending to wake up the dragons in their tummies.

I had to focus really hard to slow my breathing because my mind had started racing with all the other dangers there could be in the woods for my brothers – steep drops, a stream, barbed wire, and that's even before they started climbing trees by themselves. But I had to keep it together – Ed and Amos needed me.

We hurried off into the woods, us going left

and Dad going to the right, calling their names.

"Ed! Amos! This isn't funny and you'd better come out or you'll be in big trouble," called Shazmin. When there was no reply, she absolutely yelled, *"GET OUT HERE NOW, YOU LITTLE TERRORS!"*

I grimaced. "If they are somewhere nearby and they can hear you, threatening them with trouble probably isn't going to get them to come to us," I told her.

"Well, what would *you* do then?" she snapped, looking like she was about to cry.

"What if we can't find them?" said Bella, looking sick with anxiety.

I felt panic rising in my chest, and I thought I might be sick. I called out, in a fun voice, even though that was really hard to do: "Ed! Amos! It's time to go and get a snack with Dad. You can have the rest of those sweets that Shaz brought, and there's popcorn..."

I paused and we all listened hard. No reply. Not a single sound apart from the breeze blowing through the leaves around us and birds singing. "And we can do the hot chocolate early – we don't have to wait until it's dark!" I added. They loved hot chocolate, so that was my best shot. But ... *nothing*. I really started to panic then. So much so that I ended up shouting, "Get out here right now!" really crossly, exactly like I'd told Shazmin not to do.

GET OUT HERE RIGHT NOW!

But still nothing.

"This wood could be huge," said Bella, after we'd searched and called out for another ten minutes at least. "We'd better head back and check in with your dad. He might have found them, and we could end up getting lost ourselves."

"Speaking of lost," said Shazmin, "they could

be really far away by now, and in any direction! What if this all started off being funny to them but now they're actually lost, and scared?"

That really upset me – I know my brothers can be annoying sometimes, but I couldn't stand thinking of them somewhere in the huge wood, alone and frightened. My brain kind of gave up at that point. "I can't think properly," I croaked, my mouth dry as a desert. "I'm really scared for them but are we over-reacting? We don't even know that they're *in* the woods!"

"That's true," said Bella. "But they wanted to collect firewood, so it seems the likely option." She sighed. "Oh, I can't think clearly either."

Shazmin didn't speak at all, and just looked like she was going to be sick at any moment.

I really, really needed to take charge – they were my little brothers, after all. Suddenly I remembered… We had Breathing Magic for when we were feeling like this. As in, feeling worried or even frightened. Our adrenaline was pounding so hard through our bodies it was scrambling our brains. "Let's just take a minute to calm ourselves down," I said. "Then we can work out what to do."

Bella nodded. "Yes, please."

"OK, so breathing in, I breathe in calm," I said, just like in Kris's handout. I didn't feel calm, I felt *STRESSED OUT!* But having to lead the breathing for the others really helped me to focus. "Breathing out, I breathe out fear."

We all breathed the words in and out for a couple of minutes, thinking them to ourselves in our heads. Afterwards, Bella stamped her feet on the ground. "That's better, I can feel my

BREATHE IN …
BREATHE OUT …

legs again. I thought they were going to give way under me for a minute there."

"I had an idea, while we were doing that," said Shazmin. "If they're hiding, maybe because they're scared of getting in trouble, we could use the tracking skills we learned at the practice camp out. And if we have no luck in ten minutes, then we'll go and check in with your dad and—"

"Call the police and helicopters and sniffer dogs," said Bella, looking very worried.

"Well, probably not that, but we could drive up to the house and ask the owners to come and help us look," said Shazmin. "They'll know the land really well."

I knew we had to try her idea, for a little while at least, before raising the alarm. "OK, let's go for it," I said. "We'd better stay together. We need to get still and silent, and start listening."

So that's exactly what we did, like when we'd done the Listening in Nature in Bella's garden and written the poems. Then we slowly began to walk deeper into the woods, putting our feet down so carefully that we didn't make a sound, just like in the tracking we did with Steve. I started looking for footprints, or any evidence that Ed and Amos had been down this path. There was nothing to see for ages, and we didn't hear anything that could have been them. But I kept my breathing calm and steady, and we kept walking, and listening, and looking. And then we DID hear an unusual sound – like a twig snapping up ahead. We all turned sharply to look at one another.

"It could have been a fox or something," I whispered. "But..."

"Let's head in that direction," said Bella.

We set off again, and when the path forked and we had to choose which way to go, we followed the direction of the sound. Bella took the ribbon out of her hair and tied it to a low branch to mark the path we'd come down, so we'd be able to find our way back.

"Good thinking," I whispered.

"I'm not getting stuck out here tonight!" she hissed, with a shudder.

We carried on, looking carefully at the ground as we went, and as we reached a muddy patch Shazmin gasped and crouched low to the ground. "Look!" she whispered. She pointed to a dinosaur print, and then another and another, caught in the muddy patch.

"Amos has those prints on the bottom of his shoes!" I whispered. "Well done, Shaz, we're on the right track!" We did some silent high fives and carried on going, listening as carefully as we could to the spaces all around us. Just because we'd found the track didn't mean Ed and Amos weren't lost, of course, or that they weren't miles away by now... But it was a start.

Then – *CRACK!* – another noise. Not far away this time.

Shazmin turned and put her finger to her lips, and we hardly dared breathe. There was a rustle in a bush to our right. I felt suddenly furious with my brothers and started marching over there but Bella caught me by the arm. "Arch! If it's them and they think they're in trouble, they might take off running again," she hissed. I knew she was right, but it was really hard to stop myself from just marching up to the bush and checking.

Shazmin's eyes twinkled. "I've got an idea," she whispered. Then she said loudly, "I guess we're never going to find Ed and Amos, they're far too clever for us! Let's just have a rest here and share some interesting facts."

Bella and I were just staring at her like, *what on earth are you talking about?* But then she said, "I read the other day that a rhinoceros's bottom can turn blue if it eats too many agapanthus flowers."

There was another rustle in the bush, and I found myself grinning at Shazmin. I suddenly understood what she was up to. "I'm sure that's not true," I said loudly. "But I did hear that if you fart in space the sound comes out but because there's zero gravity the actual fart just hangs around forever like a cloud and floats around the spaceship."

"Oh no, you're wrong about that," Bella said. "Actually, the fart comes out but then it disappears – *WHOOSH!* – straight back up your bottom."

That's when we heard it, an actual giggle. The relief that went through my body was so huge – and all the terrible 'what ifs' in my mind disappeared. PHEW! I signalled that the girls should keep talking while I crept up to the bush.

"I heard that a man in Iceland broke the world

record for the longest time being set inside a jelly," said Shazmin. "He did four days in a giant orange and pineapple one – it was all over the news."

With that, there was more giggling and two coppery heads popped up from the bush. "That's impossible," said Ed. "How would he breathe?"

"Through a snorkel," said Shazmin. "And how dare you run—"

I grabbed both my brothers and held them tight so they couldn't even think about dashing off again. I hugged them hard and they hugged me back. I was just so relieved to see them that I couldn't get angry. I took their hands, one on each side, and we headed off out of the woods.

"How did he wee?" Amos asked Shazmin as we walked. "The man in the jelly?"

"Never mind that, how did he poo?" said Ed.

Shazmin couldn't help smiling then. "I guess we'll have to look it up online," she told them, with a wink at me. I smiled back at her, and then Bella gave us a big grin and a thumbs up. We'd done it! We'd found Ed and Amos and saved the camping trip – and I absolutely promised myself that I wouldn't take my eyes off them again! When we were safely back in the field, I did give them a real telling-off, though, and amazingly they did listen and say sorry – they obviously knew how serious things had been!

Dad strode out of the woods a lot further down the field just then, and he came running over when he saw that we had the twins with us. He thanked us loads for finding them and told them off a lot more than I had! They both gave him a big hug, though, and said sorry again – I think that

secretly they'd scared themselves a bit and I was
sure they wouldn't do anything like that again –
at least not for the rest of the trip! So – pretty
exciting, huh? And terrifying! We'll never forget
this trip, that's for sure!

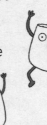

Oh, gotta go! We're toasting the rest of the
marshmallows on the fire now!

*Saturday night, in the tent. Everyone else is
fast asleep (and I can hear Dad snoring!) but
I'm wide awake!*

When we got back to the tent, we boiled up some
more water and made hot chocolate. After the
woods drama, Dad had decided to sleep in the
tent with my brothers, so he could keep an ear
and an eye on them!

It was meant to be me sleeping in with him, and
the girls with my brothers, so he said, "You don't

mind, do you, Archie? I know you wanted it to be just me and you in a tent."

"No, I don't mind," I said, and I was really surprised to find that I didn't!

And I was even more surprised at myself after we made the firepit calzones (which went really, really well this time, BTW!). Bella and Shazmin offered to take Ed and Amos into our tent to play, so I could hang out with Dad on my own, but I found that I wanted us to all be together. Wow, I never thought *that* would happen on this trip! I guess getting to spend time with Dad and remembering how much I (yes, I'll say it) LOVE my little brothers had really changed things. Even if they are the most annoying two people on the planet, *LOL!*

So we all got cosy round the fire, drinking hot chocolate and toasting marshmallows. Dad got his guitar out, which he hadn't played for months, and taught us a few songs – some Beatles and Rolling Stones hits and a funny one about space farts, which he made up for Ed and Amos when they told him what we'd said in the woods!

Afterwards we were all silent for a while, even Ed and Amos, just breathing and being together and looking up at the stars. And then an absolutely astonishing thing happened. Bella leaned in close to the fire, and poked at it with a stick until it blazed up again. And then she said, "It was a dark, dark night..."

She was telling a *ghost story*! It was brilliant, and a little bit scary, but not too scary, just the right amount of scary. Ed and Amos huddled into me and Dad, and it was really fun when she made us jump suddenly by going really, really quiet and then *LOUD* as the ghost finally appeared.

"I thought ghost stories were banned, because they scared you into hearing spooky noises all night?" I said.

"They were," she told us, with a shy smile. "But I do feel much braver since I've been doing my Breathing Magic spell all the time."

Then, as we were chatting, Ed and Amos fell asleep, sitting up, leaning on me and Dad, snoring with their mouths open.

"I'll put them to bed in a minute," said Dad.

"Aw, they look so cute!" said Shazmin.

I wrinkled up my nose. "Well, I wouldn't go that far," I said, with a smile.

Suddenly I noticed a bug crawling on Ed's jumper. It was a pretty big one and I was about to brave it and get it off before Shazmin saw it. But then she put her hand on my arm, and said, "Hang on, let me do it."

"Are you sure?" asked Bella.

Shazmin took a deep breath. "Yep, I'm going for it."

Breathing deeply, she leaned over and was about to scoop the bug off Ed's jumper, when she squealed and leaped backwards, nearly waking the twins up, and cried, "No, no, I can't do it!" She collapsed in a comical heap on the ground and groaned. "More Breathing Magic for me, I think!"

"Well done for trying, though," said Bella.

"Amazing!" I said, and then with a cheeky grin I couldn't help adding, "I'd get up off the ground, though – there are probably ten more down there." Shazmin shot up like a firework when I said that, but she laughed, and we all joined in. Then Dad scooped up Ed, and took him over to the tent.

A couple of minutes later he came back for Amos.

"This has been the most amazing camping trip ever!" I said to my friends.

"Yep, best trip ever!" said Bella.

"Yeah, best ever," echoed Shazmin.

We shared a triumphant smile between us – we didn't want to talk about our top secret Feeling Good Club business in front of Dad, but we all knew what each other was thinking – that *we did it*! We pulled off our camping trip plan, and I got to spend one-on-one time with Dad. And even better, I got to realize that I love spending time with him *and* my brothers too, all at once! Bella conquered her fear and Shazmin got a bit closer to getting over hers.

"Let's go and get ready for bed," said Bella then. "And afterwards we can get into our sleeping bags and watch a movie."

Shazmin grinned at me. "Yep, I brought the iPad with me, and a charger pack, and a choice of

three different pairs of pyjamas, and my slippers
and dressing gown and Lily the rabbit."

I sighed and shook my head in despair.
Seriously – those two!

Bella laughed. "I know it's quite a long way from
proper survival and sleeping in a hollowed-out
dead camel, Archie, but at least we're here."

I smiled at that. "I'm so glad you came," I told
them.

"Me too," said Dad, strolling back over to
the fire. "And I'm so glad you've got such great
friends, Arch."

"You're right, we *are* great," said Shazmin. "Are
you coming for a movie, Archie? It's got to be
Mamma Mia."

I shook my head. "I'll stay out here, thanks,"
I said. "If I have to watch that one more time my
head will spontaneously combust."

"Your loss, Archie!" said Shazmin cheerfully,
but Bella did a mime of her head combusting.

In that moment I felt so close to my friends. Dad was right – I am really, really lucky to have them. We're very different, but we all care so much about each other, and make each other laugh, and have fun, and that's what matters. "Goodnight, girls, and thanks for your help with the boys," said Dad.

"Any time," said Shazmin.

So then it was just me and Dad again, and we drank more hot chocolate, and toasted more marshmallows on the fire, and looked up at the stars, and talked and talked and talked, about everything under the sun.

YAWN!!! OK, I'm really going to have to go to sleep now – I did feel wide awake when I started writing but now I can hardly keep my eyes open!

Day of the Week: Sunday

Feelings I experienced today:

Sunday afternoon, back at home.
On the way home, Dad treated us
all to fish and chips (well, cheesy
chips for Bella!) and we sat on one
of the picnic benches outside and ate
every single chip even though there were loads!

YUM!

The rest of the trip was so, so, so good! I've just
got off a really long Zoom with Mum and I told
her all about it, even the part about Ed and Amos
running off into the woods (and yes, they did get
told off by her too – so that was three times!).
She was so excited to hear everything and we've
decided to go camping again when she's back – my
whole family! I can't wait to start planning that trip!

But anyway, back to the trip we just took, *LOL!*

198

Here are the highlights:

* Me and Dad got to sit up really late by the fire, stargazing and just talking about everything and nothing and it was absolutely brilliant. He told me how much he misses Mum, which I hadn't even thought about! I suppose that is quite sweet, as well as a bit slushy and romantic – *BLEUGH!!*

* Having so much fun every time anyone needed to go to the loo, because the loo was a bush! Shazmin was the most hilarious – making loads of fuss about no one coming anywhere near and squealing and throwing the whole loo roll at Ed and Amos when they sneaked up on her!

HI!

* Shazmin having another go at facing a *SPIDER* in our tent. It's almost like it knew she was the scared one, because it dropped down on a thread of web right in front of her face and kind of dangled there, probably sticking out its tongue at her – if spiders have tongues that is! I don't know, maybe they do – I'll have to find that out. She didn't touch it but she took some deep breaths and quite calmly moved away from it (and made Bella get it out for her!). Definitely an improvement!

* Telling jokes and ghost stories after the spider incident. I thought we'd stay up all night, but actually we were really tired and ended up falling asleep

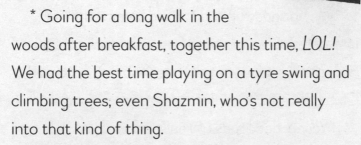

pretty quickly. I woke up to the sound of Dad whistling outside the tent – he'd got the fire going again from the embers and was cooking eggs in a pan, and toasting bread on a long fork, looking very, very pleased with himself!

* Going for a long walk in the woods after breakfast, together this time, *LOL!* We had the best time playing on a tyre swing and climbing trees, even Shazmin, who's not really into that kind of thing.

Then after some more hot chocolate, and a laze around, we got the stuff packed up and set off home. As we pulled away up the lane, I said, "I officially declare this the best camping trip ever!"

"I agree!" said Dad. "Thank you, Archie, and Bella and Shazmin, for organizing it all."

"You're welcome," said Shazmin. "It was mainly me!" Typical, *LOL!*

Then as we drove along, we sang songs all the way to the fish and chip shop!

As me and Shazmin and Bella waited outside on the picnic bench, and Dad and my bros queued up, we had a chance to talk about all the amazing things that had happened since we decided to do the Surprise Camping Trip.

"We finished turning the old summerhouse into our clubhouse – and it looks amazing!" said Shazmin. "And we did all those fab Feeling Good Club activities."

"We learned loads of really good skills while we were preparing for the camp out," said Bella. "So if there's a zombie apocalypse we will definitely survive it now."

Shazmin burst out laughing and I said, "Good to know! And you could even tell the zombies a ghost story to distract them from eating us."

Bella giggled. "Do zombies even *like* ghost stories?"

"That's something else I'm going to have to look up," I joked. "But seriously, thanks so much for all your help with the plan, guys. For me, the most important thing I've done has been…" I paused for a moment and felt all shy, but then I said, "Having that talk with Dad. Sharing my feelings and what was going on for me. It wasn't easy, but it felt really, really good, and it did actually make things better."

"That's a victory for the Feeling Good Club then!" beamed Bella. "Having our club and doing the Feeling Good activities is really helping us share our feelings and be brave!"

"I wonder what our next adventure will be?" said Shazmin. "Something fabulous, I bet!"

I smiled at that. I have no idea what's next for the Feeling Good Club, but I just know it's going to be brilliant!

Turn the page to
try out some awesome
mindfulness activities!

1.

Listening in Nature

This is a really lovely exercise to help you feel really calm, get grounded and soothe any anxious feelings swirling around in your head, chest or tummy. Some amazing magic happens as you open up and connect with the natural world around you – it just makes you feel so good!

Before you begin, try writing a few words that describe how you're feeling, or even do a drawing (if you're angry or worried, it might be a wild scribble!). Then you can do the same after Listening in Nature and see if your feelings have changed at all.

And if you like, you can get creative and write (and maybe illustrate!) your very own Listening in Nature poem too. OK, off we go…

First get your journal, or something else to write on, and a pen or pencil. Find a comfortable place to sit out in nature and take twenty minutes to simply be still and listen. You may want to close your eyes to help you focus if that feels right for you. What can you hear? Let the sounds wash over you as you breathe slowly in and out of your belly. When you've tuned in to the sound in general, you can start to listen to the different noises, one by one. You might hear birds chirping to one another, wind blowing through rustling leaves, running water or a motorbike revving its engine.

Quietly begin to write down the sounds you hear in your journal. Don't think too much about how to describe them – just note down any words and phrases that come to you. If you need a bit of help to get going, try finishing one or more of these sentences:

- The first thing I hear is…
- When I listen more deeply I hear…
- My breathing sounds like…
- When I listen for faraway sounds, I hear…
- I don't know what that sound is, but it's kind of like…
- When I'm listening in nature, I feel…

Then, after the twenty minutes is up, you could turn your notes into an amazing Listening in Nature poem!

You can illustrate your poem, or perhaps collect some things from the environment around you to decorate it. Leaf rubbings will give your page a rustic look, and so can pressed flowers – or find a friendly worm to crawl over your page, LOL! Just have fun, and don't worry about how your poem turns out!

Notice how the amazing mindfulness magic has

worked on you – do you feel calmer and more grounded? Notice how your body feels – is it more relaxed or tingly with happiness? You can write a few words about how you feel now, after the activity, and perhaps draw another picture. How are they different from what you wrote or drew before?

2.

Breathing Magic

Imagine having your own personal magic spells, with the power to banish your worries and fears! Sounds great, doesn't it? Well, guess what? You can! That's the magic of mindfulness. Grab your journal, a pen or pencil and maybe some felt tips or pencil crayons if you'd like to do some drawing too. Find yourself a quiet place where you can concentrate on creating your very own Breathing Magic… Abracadabra – worries, be gone!

So first, have a think about how you feel when you're worried or upset – what happens in your body? What physical sensations and emotions do you feel, and where do you feel them? And how about in your mind? Are there lots of thoughts racing about or just a few? There is no right or wrong answer. You can draw an outline of yourself if you like and write the thoughts, feelings and physical sensations on it, just like on a map!

Next, have a think about how you WANT to feel in your body and mind. Maybe calm, happy or brave? Perhaps you'd like to feel confident, relaxed or empowered?

Now, sit yourself down somewhere quiet if you can and start to breathe into your belly. If it helps, place your hand on your belly so you can feel it going out on the in breath and naturally moving away from your hand again on the out breath. After a few breaths, say these words to yourself, in your head or out loud, as you breathe:

- Breathing in, I breathe in calm…
- Breathing out, I breathe out worries…

Do this a few times and see if you feel any calmer.

Now, you can try saying:

- Breathing in, I breathe in courage…
- Breathing out, I breathe out fear…

Again, notice how you feel after a few rounds of this one – hopefully as brave as a lion!

You can even make up your own words, like your own personal magic spell!

- Breathing in, I breathe in _____

- Breathing out, I breathe out _____

- Breathing in, I breathe in _____

- Breathing out, I breathe out _____

There are so many words to choose from.
Remember, your words are right for you, and you

can't get it wrong! Trust that you know the right words to help yourself … and have fun!

You can write your Breathing Magic spells on a big piece of paper with fun illustrations if you like, and put them where you can see them often. And do remember, it's wonderful to have lots of tools to help yourself, but you don't have to deal with big worries or fears on your own. Telling a trusted grown-up how you're feeling is very important, so be brave and share your worries and fears with them too.

3.

Two Ways of Mindful Walking

Silly Walking

Silly Walking is a great way to get less self-conscious, loosen up and have more fun! It's also a brilliant activity to do to help you take your mind off worries, or to give you a lift if you're feeling sad. Of course, it won't magically solve your problems, but lifting your mood can really help you feel better about things, and perhaps to even get inspired with some great solutions!

Grab some friends to do this with, to make it even more fun. You can walk in any silly way you like – the sillier the better. Take the silliness up in stages, with a walk for each – maybe even creating ten levels of silliness. Go from 1. Not Silly At All to 10. Top Level Silliness. You could take turns with your friends to create sillier and sillier walks and then have a go at trying out each others' inventions. Here are some ideas to get you started:

- Create a Silly Walk that includes a hop and a skip, or some breakdancing!

- How about a walk that can only go backwards and sideways?

- Can you walk like a robot, a pirate, a hippopotamus or a tightrope walker? How about a robot pirate, or a hippo on a tightrope?

Put on some music if you like, for even more fun!

The sillier your walk is, the more you'll need all your focus and attention in the present moment – just so that you don't fall over! It's fine (and totally normal!) to feel embarrassed or self-conscious at first! Just notice where you're feeling it in your body, and if there are any thoughts darting around your mind like, 'Am I looking too silly?' or 'Am I funny enough?'. Becoming aware of our thoughts and feelings without getting too caught up in them can help them to move on through us, like passing weather.

Happy Silly Walking! Have fun!

Silent Walking

For the Silent Walking … well, you've guessed it!
With this one, you're going to walk as silently as
possible, LOL! Sssssssshhhhhh! You might think
that's pretty easy – until you try it! You'll have to
put your feet down really slowly and carefully. You
might become aware of all the muscles, tendons
and bones in your feet – and just how incredibly
amazing feet are! You can pretend you're a spy or
a ninja, or that you're tracking animals out in the
wild. Remember, try not to leave any trail behind
you! You could even get some friends together
and take turns to Silent Walk across crunchy
leaves or creaky old floorboards – and if you're
near the coast it's great fun to play on a pebbly
beach!

Enjoy!

Hi, I'm Kelly, the author of this book. I love writing (I've written

sixty books now!), horses, being out in nature, dancing, chocolate and

of course, hanging out with my friends. I also really love mindfulness

and meditation, and I wish I'd had a club like Bella, Archie and

Shazmin's when I was their age — I would have especially loved

the baking! You can find some more creative and fun mindfulness

activities on my website, and info on my books, at

www.kellymckain.co.uk — come and say hi,

it would be great to see you there!

Hi! My name is Jenny and I illustrated this awesome book. I absolutely love drawing and it's my favourite thing to do... I have even been told by my parents that I had a crayon in my hand before I could walk! Drawing makes me feel calm and has helped me in many ways throughout my life. I wish I had books like this when I was younger — I especially love how creative Archie, Bella and Shazmin are and how they get up to so many fun things together. In this book they all go camping which reminded me of how much I used to love going on camping holidays when I was younger! I loved being with nature and finding all sorts of wildlife!

I hope you love this book as much as I loved illustrating it.

To see more of my work please visit my website lathamsillustrations.com

SMASH YOUR WORRIES, BELLA!

That class talk keeps creeping into my mind and taking over...

GO AWAY, BIG WORRY!

Bella isn't looking forward to Feeling Good Week at school. Her best friend Rosh has just moved away and on top of that she has a **Big Worry** – it's her turn to do the class talk and she's *dreading* it.

But when she befriends classmates Shazmin and Archie things start to look up. Can they help Bella to smash her worries for good?

Join Bella, Archie and Shazmin as they form the Feeling Good Club and help each other to feel good, face their worries and practise some awesome mindfulness activities!

KELLY MCKAIN

THE FEELING GOOD CLUB

SMASH YOUR WORRIES, BELLA!

ILLUSTRATED BY
JENNY LATHAM

Look out for the next
Feeling Good Club book, coming soon...

BE KIND, SHAZMIN!

Sometimes I miss the old Charita so much it makes my stomach hurt.

GNURGH!

Shazmin's really upset that her teenage sister doesn't want to hang out with her any more, but she's keeping her feelings hidden from Bella and Archie. Then her plan to make Charita like her again backfires – and her unkind behaviour causes a rift with her friends.

Can Bella and Archie help Shazmin to open up about her sister and find a way to put things right?

Join in with the Feeling Good Club as Shazmin, Bella and Archie help each other to feel good, face their worries and practise some awesome mindfulness activities!

KELLY MCKAIN

THE FEELING GOOD CLUB

BE KIND, SHAZMIN!

ILLUSTRATED BY
JENNY LATHAM